For Mum and Dad,
who taught me to never give up

More books by Larry Hayes

How to Survive Without Grown-Ups
How to Survive Time Travel

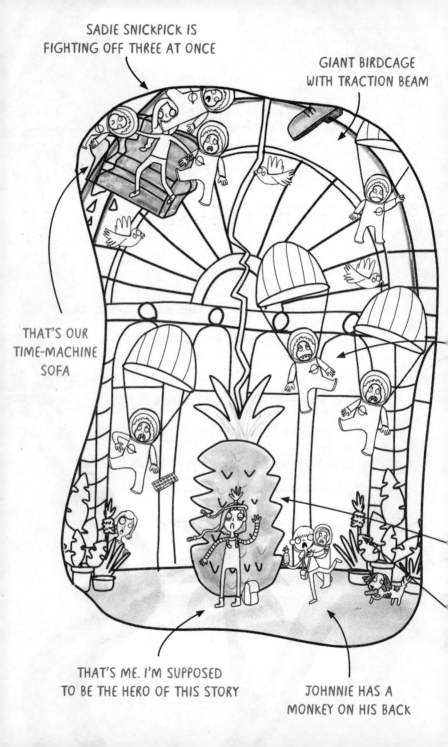

HOW TO SURVIVE THE FUTURE

LARRY HAYES

KATIE ABEY

First published in Great Britain in 2023 by Simon & Schuster UK Ltd

1 3 5 7 9 10 8 6 4 2

Simon & Schuster UK Ltd
1st Floor, 222 Gray's Inn Road
London
WC1X 8HB

www.simonandschuster.co.uk
www.simonandschuster.com.au
www.simonandschuster.co.in

Simon & Schuster Australia, Sydney
Simon & Schuster India, New Delhi

A CIP catalogue record for this book is available from the British
Library.

PB ISBN 978-1-4711-9838-0
eBook ISBN 978-1-4711-9839-7
eAudio ISBN 978-1-3985-1991-6

Printed and bound by CPI Group (UK) Ltd, Croydon, CR0 4YY

MIX
Paper | Supporting
responsible forestry
FSC® C171272
www.fsc.org

PROLOGUE
A LONG TIME IN
THE FUTURE

It's a long time in the future, the year 2525 to be exact. And things are bad.

AN INFINITE NUMBER OF
SPACE MONKEYS ARE ATTACKING
PLANET EARTH

You're probably wondering what I'm doing here. My name is Eliza Lemon and I'm stuck in a giant birdcage being attacked by space monkeys who are trying to destroy all the life on Earth.

THAT'S NOT A REAL PINEAPPLE. IT'S
A FAKE PINEAPPLE THAT CONTAINS THE
GALAXY'S SMALLEST BLACK HOLE

THAT'S JUST A
NORMAL PINEAPPLE.

1

My baby brother, Johnnie, has it worse. He's trying to save the planet using a fake pineapple that contains the galaxy's smallest black hole. Trust me, it requires some very difficult maths to pull that off.

Johnnie faces a triple threat:

SUCKED INTO A BLACK HOLE

+

MONKEY ON HIS BACK

+

VERY DIFFICULT MATHS = TRIPLE THREAT

You're probably worried about us. You're probably a bit tearful, thinking, What a waste of money! This book will be really short if they get sucked into a black hole right at the start.

But don't cry, not yet. Save your tears for when you really need them. I learned this the hard way earlier today. Just before lunch.

HOW NOT TO CRY
(THE HARD WAY)

I used to cry all the time.

Then I just stopped. I ran out of tears. I'm not completely sure why.

I lost my parents, but that wasn't it. The thing that made me cry so much that I ran out of tears was finding them again.

Hold on, that sounds weird. I need to explain this properly, otherwise you'll think I'm weird.

OK, I am weird, but I want you to think I'm weird for the right reasons, not the wrong ones, so let me back up a bit and explain exactly what happened.

I was born in the year 2042, just after the

northern ice cap melted, and for ten years my life was pretty normal. All right, my teacher used to bully me – that's not completely normal.

Mrs Crosse writes 'Loser' on my forehead at Register.

She deliberately spells it wrong too. IT'S SO HUMILIATING.

And then she washes it off at the end of the day so my parents won't believe me. I HOPE YOU AGREE this is not normal behaviour for a teacher.

And my PE teacher, Mr Murray, spent five years trying to kill me. Yes, actually kill me actually dead. Which no one ever believes, so I guess that's not normal either.

Mr Murray glues lego to the school trampoline. Who does that? Why would you do that???

You'd be put off exercise too.

But worse than them. Worse than anyone in the history of the world. Worse, even, than that guy who invented SATS, was Sadie.

SADIE SNICKPICK.

The meanest person ever to live on Planet Earth. I could handle a hundred Mrs Crosses and a thousand Mr Murrays if I could only get away from

Sadie Snickpick is the world's biggest bully.
She even has her own 'how to' YouTube channel.
We're not just talking about the odd wedgie.
We're talking:

If you don't know what any of these mean, then
lucky you. You've never met Sadie Snickpick.

Sadie-the-Sadist-Snickpick. Even grown-ups were scared of her. And Sadie, for some reason I've never totally understood, declared me ENEMY NUMBER ONE on our first day of school. She's spent the last five years making sure my life is a living hell.

So when I say 'The first ten years of my life were normal', I don't mean normal-normal. I mean normal compared to what happened next.

What happened next was freaky. (You really should read the books.[1]

There's a lot of good stuff in there about how to survive all sorts of things, and they're so laugh-out-loud funny some teachers actually fart out loud when they're reading them to their class, which is kind of memorable). In case you can't be bothered with all the laughing and farting, I can just draw a picture to sum up the story so far:

---

1 *How to Survive Without Grown-Ups* and *How to Survive Time Travel.*

Basically, about three months ago, right in the middle of summer term, a super-billionaire called Noah tried to set up life on Mars and he took two of every animal into his space ark, including my mum and dad. Me, Johnnie (my little brother) and Myrt (our dog) stopped him, obvs, but then Mum and Dad, being total idiot grown-ups, started fiddling around with Noah's time machine and got sucked back 7,000 years to ancient Egypt.

That was bad, but then it got worse. Johnnie fixed up another time machine (did I mention he's only five years old but he's a total genius?[2]) and we went back to ancient Egypt to rescue Mum and Dad – but ended up having to save the world from Noah a second time. To make it even worse, Sadie came with us by mistake (which was really awkward), but it turns out having a total savage bully on your side can be really useful. And, to be honest, I don't think we could have done without her.

But, worst of all, in the process of saving the world, my dad got trapped in a freezer and my mum got stuck in a cave in the middle of the Sahara Desert.

---

2   Johnnie is a **total** genius, which is really annoying. My mum ate loads of sardine sandwiches when she was pregnant and so Johnnie got this massive brain. He makes Wikipedia look thick. So you can imagine how I feel.

So now I've got a dad who is literally cold and unfeeling. And a mum who's literally stuck in the past.

Well, she was the last time I saw her. Which was 5000 BCE. I'm not sure what she is now. I'd do anything to get my mum and dad back, and every time I thought about it I wanted to hug Myrt and have a cry.

But that was this morning, when I still had some tears left in me.

Since then everything just got a bucketload worse.[3]

Before I go on, I need to explain one more thing. We saved the world by using the time machine. We used it to teleport tons of gunpowder so Noah couldn't blow up the planet. It also teleported us – me, Johnnie, Myrt and Sadie – to safety. Except something went wrong.

I can remember the time machine doing its thing – it kind of rubs everything out like a giant eraser – but before it got to me and Myrt . . . Well, I can remember the heat from the gunpowder as it blasted us backwards, and then everything went black. When I woke up, we were here:

---

3   We're talking a bucketload of cat vomit here, people.

Imagine being trapped in a cube of white jelly that just squidges if you kick it. It's also really bright, like a light box, but if you say, 'Lights off' the light goes off and it's really dark.

When I first woke up I was just glad to be alive. After all, I had been in a huge man-made volcano that was a nanosecond away from turning me into a ball of plasma, so basically anything was an upgrade.[4] But after a breakfast of lentils I was starting to feel less happy, so I did what I always do when I'm worried – I dug a new notebook out of my rucksack and started this journal.

Besides, just before lunch (more lentils!), the cube went see-through and I could suddenly see the world around me, and it looked amazing. My jelly cube was in a beautiful park with neatly mown grass. It was like the entire world had become one giant perfect lawn. And there were loads of other cubes – like little houses, each with one person inside playing computer games. There were trees too, all covered in bright pink blossom, and, beyond

---

4   Yep, it's all in *How to Survive Time Travel*. In case you're still not convinced, it's got some really good learning points, like, 'How to Jump out of a Tree', 'How to Become a God' and 'How to Wipe the Smile off your Brother's Face'. There is even a bit about fighting someone with a Brussels sprout. This is stuff you can't learn in school.

them, a giant white statue – so tall its head was lost in the clouds.

High above everything was a shiny steel doughnut – yes, a doughnut – hovering in the sky like a giant doughnut advert with a stream of red light beaming down to Earth like a long thread of jam.

Taking all this in, it didn't take much brainpower to realize two important things:

IMPORTANT THING 1. Something must have gone truly badly wrong with our time machine because I'd been catapulted into the Far, Far Future.

IMPORTANT THING 2. The Far, Far Future was pretty strange.

STRANGE FLYING
DOUGHNUT

STRANGELY MASSIVE
STATUE OF SOMEBODY

And then something super-freaky-weird happened.

Alongside my lunch, on the tray, was a letter, and the letter was from Johnnie. I'll just stick it in so you can read it for yourself. It's basically the saddest thing you'll ever read.

Wibbly Cottage,

Lower Biscuit

4th Sept 2053

Hi Eliza,

I hope you're OK. So, good news about saving the world. I'm back home and it's just like we left it. Which is a bit of a mess, to be honest.

It's weird being on my own. Dad's here, obviously, but I haven't managed to defrost him yet. It all looks a LOT more complicated than we thought. I'm sure he'll be all right, but I just want to make absolutely sure I'm doing it right and there's not much on the internet about how to defrost your frozen dad.

It's my first day at school tomorrow and I don't want to go. But if I don't go then they'll send someone round to the house and figure out that

Dad's frozen and everything. I'm trying to get the sofa fixed so I can go and rescue Mum like you said, but it's pretty bashed up. I don't know if I can do it without you. I don't know if I can do anything without you, 'Liza. Why can't you just come back?

You said Sadie would look after me, but she just went off on her bike as soon as we got here. And now I don't know what to do. I'm scared. Why can't you just come home? I know you survived the volcano – I saw you and Myrt being scanned. How did you do that, BTW? You must have hit the volume button A LOT because it scanned a ton of gunpowder as well. Most of it's still on the lawn, but I don't know where you and Myrt went, or when you went, or why you didn't just come back here.

Anyhow, I've figured out how to copy this letter using what's left of the time machine and I'm going to copy it a zillion times and send it to every year all the way out to the Year 3000. If you get it, please write back; there's loads of things I'm not sure about. Like where you get school uniform from and where you go after you get to the school gates and how do you order lunch?

   Lots of love, Eliza, and see you soon,

   Johnnie

   x x x x

       x

       x

   x x x

So that's how I know Johnnie got back home to the year 2053. I tasted sick in my throat at the thought of his first day of school – the thought of him having to face Mrs Crosse and all the rest of them alone. No Mum, Dad still frozen, me and Myrt stuck here – wherever (and whenever) here is. I wanted to cry, but for some reason I couldn't. Not a single tear. And that's when I realized – tears are no use if there's no one to see them. No one to dry them or kiss them away. When nobody cares about you, tears are just silly.

But Johnnie's letter wasn't even the super-freaky-weird thing.

The super-freaky-weird-thing was *the person who brought the letter.* He looked exactly like Mr Murray, my PE teacher.

You know, the one who's been trying to kill me for the last five years.

HOW TO GET OUT OF PE

Now, you probably think all PE teachers are a bit deadly. They make you run and they get annoyed when you don't look like you're enjoying tag rugby in January. You probably think the worst PE teachers are the ones who 'join in' so they can win.[5]

Yes, they're pretty bad, but, no, they're not the worst. The worst PE teachers are actually **out to kill you.** Like this:

---

5   Why do all PE teachers have to show off about how good they are at sport? Come on, PE teachers, you're big strong adults; we're small and weak because we look at screens all day so our muscles haven't developed. You grew up when computer games were rubbish and so running about seemed fun. Give your sports trophies a polish and get over yourselves.

MR MURRAY LOOKALIKE ATTACK

Then he left. With a smile. And not a word.

And Myrt and me? Well, we spent the afternoon trapped in our jelly cube.

It felt like we'd been there for ever, and I should have hated it. I should have been pacing and nail-biting, worrying about Johnnie and the Mr Murray lookalike. Or was he the actual Mr Murray? If so, then what was he doing here in the future?? Or was he a twin?? And – most of all – I should have been planning how to rescue my mum and dad.

I sat back with Myrt on my lap and wrote in my journal. I thought it might help me make sense of everything, and I was determined to come up with a plan. But instead I got distracted by that strange view of the far future, and as the sun slowly sank towards the horizon, we mainly just sat there, gawping in wonder.

The huge statue was the really curious thing. The somebody was holding up a pineapple, which was

just weird, and in their other hand was a nunchuck –
or maybe a skipping rope – which was even weirder.
And it was all so tall that the head was stuck in the
clouds. I spent ages waiting for the clouds to part so
I could check out the face. But they never did.

The other thing was the doughnut. The giant silver
doughnut hovering high in the sky, practically in
space. Sunshine sparkled off it like an artificial
moon, and a beam of red light fell to Earth like a

massive gloop of jam. If it was a giant doughnut advert, then it was a good one, because all afternoon I couldn't stop thinking about jammy doughnuts.

After looking at all that for what felt like hours, 'Mr Murray' was suddenly back, stepping into my cube with a plate of green spaghetti and a smile beneath his bristly moustache.

I was immediately on edge.

I watched him carefully as he bent down to collect my lunch plate. And then the man who has spent the last five years trying kill me . . . tried to kill me again.

The empty plate came flying at me like a killer Frisbee.

It was metal and I ducked, but it bit into the wall above my head and got lodged in the hard jelly.

Then a fork came flying out of his other hand, and at that moment, as the prongs came at my left eyeball, I made two decisions.

DECISION 1: I HAD TO GET OUT OF HERE QUICK.

AND

DECISION 2: I'D HAD ENOUGH OF MR MURRAY. AND HIS LOOKALIKE.

I'd had enough of having stuff thrown at me. Balls, cones and beanbags. He even threw another kid at me once. Anything you can throw, he'd thrown at me. I tell you, it's not normal, even for a PE teacher.

Big-moustachioed-muscleman he might be, but it was time to fight back.

The fork flew through the air, but for once I didn't duck. I didn't dodge.

I just caught it.

'You're a grown man – stop it. STOP IT!' I shouted.

A string of spaghetti came next; it hit me in the face and something just snapped. I pulled my arm back and did something I never thought I'd do in a million years.

I threw the fork straight back at him.

Right at his chest.

Well, I aimed at his chest, but I've never been much of thrower.[6]

6   What do you expect? My PE lessons have been totally inadequate. I can throw a netball long distance – but that's about it. And that's only because Mr Murray always makes

I'd only meant to distract him and then run for it, but as the fork flew it began to veer higher and in total horror I saw it hit him – right in his face.

Right in the moustache.

It stuck there, quivering. And he looked a bit cross-eyed and angry. He was twice my size, easy. He just tugged at the fork like he couldn't even feel it.

'I'm so sorry. I didn't mean t—' That's all I managed to say before he yanked it free.

In that moment everything I thought I knew about the world was turned upside down and inside out.

---

me play on a team of one.

I don't wanna think about it, let alone write about it. And I don't even know if I've got the words to describe what happened.

Probably best I just draw it. Cos Mr Murray's magnificent moustache? Well, it just came clean off – along with the fork.

And so did the rest of his face.

BEFORE   AFTER

Suddenly it made sense – how Mr Murray could be both here in the far future and in the past. Mr Murray wasn't a human. He was some kind of robot.

I screamed and Myrt barked.

And then the bot came at me, lunging mechanically with his moustachioed fork.

This Mr Murray, it seemed, had been programmed to kill.

HOW TO FIGHT A
KILLER ROBOT

Myrt saved me. She ran at the MurrayBot's leg and bit down. And she just wouldn't let go – Myrt never lets go. He dragged her along, but she slowed him down. Crucially this gave me time to pull the plate from the wall behind me.

I chucked it at his circuit-board face and sparks flew. Then the bot stopped and slumped like a puppet with cut strings.

I looked at Myrt, still biting down on his leg. I couldn't believe it. After all these years of being attacked, I'd finally defeated my PE teacher.

And then robot's eyes whirred back open with a click, and its head lifted up.

Level 1: Reaction training complete . . . Level 2: Mantis attack sequence commence.

Mantis attack?

As in kung fu??

This just didn't make sense.

Until suddenly it did.

Suddenly I knew exactly what I was facing.

Suddenly the last five years of PE misery made total sense. Mr Murray wasn't a PE teacher. He wasn't even a robot PE teacher. Mr Murray was a **combat-training bot**, like the ones they use in the army.

And this was gonna get ugly.

Kung fugly.

His hands stiffened, turning into weapons, and they moved in beautiful fluid arcs. Myrt looked up at him, then bit down harder. The MurrayBot tried to kick her off, but Myrt locked her jaws. And when Myrt's jaws are locked, they're immovable.

The MurrayBot's kung fu hands were moving so fast they were just a blur.

Behind him the door was still open, an escape. But an escape to what? What kind of future was I escaping to?

For a moment I hesitated – frozen with fear. But then I did the only sensible thing a ten-year-old can do when facing an out-of-control **combat-training bot**.

I ran.

I ran past him in terror, right on to that giant lawn.

I ran as fast as I could, right into the future.

HOW TO RUN INTO
THE FUTURE

I didn't know it then, but I was in the year 2525, almost 500 years after I'd been born.

And in the year 2525 they have really nice springy lawns.

I leapt on to the grass and felt it bounce under my feet. The sky was darkest blue, the kind of blue you only see in other people's holiday photos, but I was too busy to think about any of that. I didn't even think about Myrt stuck in the cube with that mad robot.

I had no idea where I was going – I just ran. Anything to get away from the MurrayBot. And, for some reason, I ran towards the giant statue and the sea.

The statue seemed bigger now; its knees were above the trees, bright white above the pink blossoms. As I ran the wind blew and a rain of blossom filled the air, hiding me in its pink embrace.

Eventually the grass gave way to gravel – but I still didn't look back, terrified of what I'd see. The gravel was raked into beautiful swirling patterns, like a zen garden, but I didn't care – I just crunched right over it, messing up the lines. A voice shouted from somewhere, but I ignored it. Nothing was going to stop me. Not with that robot after me.

Or so I thought.

Because just then, as I reached the statue looking for somewhere to hide, I realized my mistake. The statue backed on to the edge of a cliff, with only the sea and the sun beyond it. I'd literally run out of road.

The only way out was to jump off a cliff.

HOW TO JUMP OFF
A CLIFF

Now, if you've read my earlier journals, you'll know that we live on the edge of a cliff. We've even got a slide into the sea. And you'll also know that I've only gone down it once and that I'll never, ever do it again.

That was the thought that flashed through my brain as I stood there, desperately looking for somewhere to run. But I never did, because suddenly I could hear a voice behind me. A kind voice that finished in a chuckle, a little-old-man chuckle.

'If you could stop messing up the sunflower seeds, I'd be very grateful.'

I turned and saw the oldest little old man you've

even seen. He was smaller than me and looked like he'd been sun-dried for about a million years.

Imagine a tomato, and then imagine a sun-dried tomato – now imagine the same thing happening to a human being.

'Hello,' the old man said. 'I'm Karlos.'

He leaned on an old garden rake as if it was the only thing holding him up.

I looked down at the mess I'd made of his gravel. But now I looked properly, I saw it wasn't normal gravel. Each little stone was shaped and coloured like a sunflower seed.

I bent to pick one up, my brain still tumbling about, but then a loud crunch stopped me dead. The MurrayBot was storming through the trees and on to the gravel. He saw me and smiled. And then he started to run.

'You've gotta help,' I shouted. 'That robot's trying to kill me!'

'Well done,' said the old man, his eyes disappearing with a huge smile, 'you finally levelled up.' He went back to his raking.

'You don't understand! *It wants to kill me!*'

The MurrayBot was running fast, and that's when I saw Myrt still clinging on to its leg, being battered with every step.

Little Myrt. She'd clung on with her teeth, and I'd left her.

My stomach heaved.

I managed not to vom, but I knew, as I hunched over, that I couldn't run away any more. I'd been running all my life – from bullies at school, from teachers who wanted to make my life a misery. Running, running, running. The sound of the MurrayBot on gravel filled my ears. Every step battering Myrt's little body.

Looking at her little face, I knew what I had to do.

The running away had to stop.

HOW TO STOP
RUNNING AWAY

It sounds simple but it's not.

Not when you've spent a lifetime running away from stuff (like *everystuff*: the ball in PE, Sadie Snickpick, school plays, play dates . . . I even ran away from my own sixth birthday party [7] twice[8]).

I looked at the old man. He was still smiling, like he was either really stupendously wise or really stupendously stupid. I wasn't sure which so I just grabbed his rake.

It was wide, wooden and weighty. The perfect weapon.

---

7   Sadie Snickpick put half a cat poo in the middle of the pass-the-parcel parcel and then let me win.

8   She put the other half in my party bag.

So I ran, but this time I didn't run away. I ran towards. I ran at the MurrayBot and I didn't stop until I'd slammed the head of the rake into its belly.

And then – I couldn't believe it – the robot body just popped apart. The body flew into the air with the *satisfying crunch of metal on metal*. For a few moments, the legs just stood there, all on their own. And then they tipped backwards on to the gravel.

I looked down at them, at the wires springing everywhere. Myrt was still clinging on with her teeth. She looked tiny; all her fur was matted down with blood – her blood.

But there was no time to do anything about it, because the *MurrayBot body pulled itself up*. I watched in horror as it lifted itself up on to its arms, and slowly, using its arms as legs, walked towards me.

I swung with my rake and one of its robot arms flew off. But even with one arm it just kept going, dragging itself over the gravel.

I knew then that it would never stop.

It couldn't be bargained with. It couldn't be reasoned with. It absolutely would not stop . . . EVER until I was dead.

I looked into its dark robot eyes and jabbed down, but it caught the rake, just grabbed it, and started pulling. Gadz, it was strong, even with only one hand. I just couldn't hold on.

'You know you can stop him whenever you want?' The old man's voice was calm. The robot yanked the rake out of my hands and I turned in panic.

'*What?!*'

'All robots have a failsafe. Just use its name.'

I looked blank.

'*Colin* Murray,' he said as the MurrayBot swung the rake at me, 'stop.'

The MurrayBot stopped. The eyelids closed, the head flopped and the whole thing collapsed on to the gravel. Karlos gave me a little shrug and a smile.

Five years of PE misery, of bruises, cuts, humiliation and pain – and that's all it took. Three words: **Colin Murray, stop**.

But how on earth was I expected to know Mr Murray's first name was 'Colin'? And who calls anybody '*Colin*'?[9] But there wasn't time to think about of that.

'Myrt!!' I screamed, and ran to her. Her jaws were still clamped round the MurrayBot's left leg, her lungs were pumping fast and so was the blood. There was just so much blood and I didn't have the first idea what to do.

Myrt, the dog with nine lives, was about to lose her last one.

---

9 **Editor's footnote**: The publishers wish to apologize in advance to any readers called Colin. All names have value, even Geoffrey, Larry and Doris; you should never be ashamed of your name. Names simply go in and out of fashion – so depending on when you're reading this, Colin may or may not be cool. And you can always change it by deed poll when you're eighteen.

HOW TO GET A TENTH LIFE

The fur round her neck was stuck flat with blood. I pressed down hard to stop it, but the blood kept coming, seeping through my fingers. Gooey puddles of it. Soaking the gravel a hideous crimson red.

Myrt's little body felt tiny. It looked tiny with all the fur stuck down. I picked her up and she weighed nothing. And with her heart thumping and the blood pumping I finally shouted.

A shout so loud Johnnie probably heard it in 2053. Myrt looked up at me and softly chewed my hand. A feeble little bite. I shut my eyes and suddenly my mind was sucked through time and space to when I was a baby – and Myrt was a little puppy, chewing on my arm as I giggled at the tickle.

And then I was back. On the sunflower-seed gravel in the year 2525, and Myrt was still in my arms, still bleeding. But the old man was kneeling and he was speaking with a kind voice.

'Not to worry,' he said, 'we just stop the bleeding.'

HOW TO STOP THE BLEEDING

You don't need *The Book of Secrets*[10] for this one. Any old first-aid book will do.

In the past, when my mum was growing up, they used something called a 'plaster'. They sound kind of gross. Basically, they were like fake scabs that came off in swimming pools. In my day (the year 2053), Mum and Dad had a glue gun for cuts and stuff, but I guess things had moved on by 2525.

The old man pulled out a pen. He clicked it a couple of times and then sort of scribbled in the air

---

10 If you don't know what *The Book of Secrets* is, you have to check it out – it basically contains all the things kids need to know that grown-ups don't tell them. Like How to Get Sweets for Breakfast, How to Tell if Someone's Lying and How to Win a Dance Battle. That sorta thing.

THE BOOK
OF SECRETS
A BAJILLION
THINGS GROWN-UPS
DON'T WANT YOU
TO KNOW

over Myrt's neck.

'What are you doing?' I said suspiciously.

'Please wait,' he said in his slow old-man voice.

So I waited with Myrt on my lap as the old man worked with his pen. She fell asleep, and for a bit I still thought she might die, but the pulse in her belly never missed a beat.

After a few moments Karlos took off his silk scarf and made me a little sling. He placed it over my shoulder and we slid Myrt inside.

'There,' he said, 'now you can carry her around until she recovers.'

'So, what do you think of your statue?' he asked matter-of-factly.

I looked at him and his eyes flicked upwards.

The clouds had cleared, and, believe it or not, that's the first time I saw all of it.

It must have been 200 metres high. The stone was bleached so white by the sunlight that it hurt my eyes to look at it. I squinted, trying to take it all in. 'My statue?'

'Yes, Eliza Lemon – you can be seen from space.'

Myrt wriggled on my lap. 'What do you mean?'

But he didn't answer. He didn't need to. He just nodded towards the base of the statue. Letters had been carved into the stone there. Giant letters each one taller than me.

I read them slowly, my brain tumbling about in my head. Nothing made sense, because those letters spelled out the last thing you'd ever guess.

They spelled out my name:

ELIZA LEMON

And immediately it was obvious.

It *was* my statue.

It was a statue of *me*.

'You've probably got some questions,' said the old man.

And I did.

I definitely did.

ELIZA THE COLOSSUS

Why am I holding a pineapple?

Why do I look so gormless?

What's with all the birds??

Is that a nunchuck or a skipping rope?

HOW TO GET SOME
ANSWERS

Now if you've ever seen a 200-metre-high statue of yourself, you'll know one thing.

It's a bit creepy seeing yourself with a nose that big. And my ears! They were as big as bungalows.

'What's with the nunchuck?' I asked Karlos.

'We're fairly sure it's a skipping rope.' He tapped his fingers on the wooden handle of the rake. 'Though scholars have been arguing about that for over four hundred years.'

'Four hundred years?'

But that wasn't the question. None of these questions was the question – the question I really wanted to ask, the question I needed to ask was just:

But for some reason I hesitated.

'I expect you want to know why there's a statute of you in the year 2525 that's so big it can be seen from space. Biscuit?'

'Yes.' I nodded energetically and he gave me a biscuit. Myrt whimpered in her sling, as if she could smell it in her dream.

'It's kind of a warning.'

'What is?'

'It is. You is. You are . . . You're a warning to the galaxy.'

What? Me? How?? I had my pick of questions, but

my mouth just flopped open. Sometimes in life it's best to just let your mouth flop open and listen.

'This statue is a warning to the galaxy – to let them know the Earth is protected. That we have a **Guardian**.'

'A Guardian?' Tingles went up my chest. He meant me. And if you thought my mouth was floppy before, you should have seen it then. Because in that moment – like an out-of-control nightmare – I could see that the entire human race

had made one

giant,

colossal,

humongous,

200-metre-tall **mistake**.

'I think you've made a mistake,' I said in a small voice. 'I think you've mixed me up with somebody else.'

HOW TO SORT OUT
A BIG MISTAKE

People make mistakes all the time. Some are small (beef-flavoured crisps), some are big (forgetting your PE kit and having to do it in your pants), some are very big (like forgetting to wear pants on the day you forget your PE kit). And then there are the truly ginormous ones like anchovies on pizza and Mondays.

But this put them all in the shade.

For some horribly jumbled bit of history that I'll probably never understand, the super-advanced human beings of 2525 had decided that they didn't need to worry about being invaded by aliens because I – me, Eliza Lemon – was somehow going to save them.

I felt like vomming for a second time that afternoon. Then, to make things worse, jelly cubes started arriving – each one with a kid inside. The cubes oozed across the gravel while the kids just sat there.

One by one the cubes of kids circled us.

'What are they doing?' I asked nervously, but Karlos just waved a hand.

'Don't worry about them – they've just come to get a better look at you.'

And, as if to prove it, their faces began to pop on to the cubes – giant faces projected on to the cube wall – all the better to get a good gawp at me. Like I was some new spectator sport.

Then the cubes began stacking up – one on top of the other to make a giant jelly wall – each brick a huge gawking face. None of them looked more than eleven years old.

It was creepy and getting creepier by the minute.

'Why are they just sitting there?' I asked.

Karlos pulled a face. 'Everybody gave up standing centuries ago. Video games just got too good.'

'But what about you?' I said, finishing off my biscuit.

'I don't like video games,' he said. 'I guess that's why they made me president of the planet.'

I'd never met a president before – let alone a world president. I wondered whether to salute or bow or something, but all the while the cubes were gathering and the wall growing higher.

'Just try to ignore them,' Karlos said simply. 'Have another biscuit and I'll catch you up on a few hundred years of history.'

I took another biscuit.

This was one history lesson I needed to stay awake for.

HOW TO STAY AWAKE DURING A HISTORY LESSON

Now, I don't know about you, but I generally fall asleep in history. There's something nice and cosy and sleepifying about learning about stuff that's already happened. Nothing can really go wrong in history. You don't need to stress or worry about anyone because you already know the ending: **Everyone Dies**.

'OMG! Nice chariot, Boudicca, but what will happen when you fight the Romans?'

'She dies.'

'Oh no, it's so tense. What will happen to Anne Boleyn now Henry VIII thinks she's a witch??'

'She dies.'

'Oooh, Napoleon – he's gone crazy-pants, invading everywhere. What's gonna happen???'

'He dies.'

But history's a whole different ball game when you don't know how it ends. Especially when you're the main character. It's basically terrifying.

The first thing the old man did was show me the rest of the inscription at the bottom of the statue.

COMETH THE HOUR, COMETH THE GIRL
HERE LIE THE BONES OF ELIZA LEMON
SAVIOUR OF PLANET EARTH IN THE YEAR 2525

'Saviour of Planet Earth?' I shook my head. 'I don't get it.'

Now, I don't want to brag about it, but maybe I did save the world once before, but that was just dumb luck. And it was mainly Sadie if I'm honest. She was the one who kicked the sherbet lemon into Noah's eyeball.[11] But that was, like, 5000 BCE.

The old man drummed his fingers on the rake handle. It was beginning to distract me, but I

---

11 If you could just read *How to Survive Time Travel*, then I won't have to keep explaining this stuff.

didn't say anything.

'We don't get it either. But **the computer** predicted it, and you don't argue with **the computer**.'

'The computer?'

'It's what we call . . . this. He waved his hand at the cubes. They were still building higher, crowding over us like a giant igloo dome of jelly cubes.

In case that doesn't make sense,
this is what it looked like:

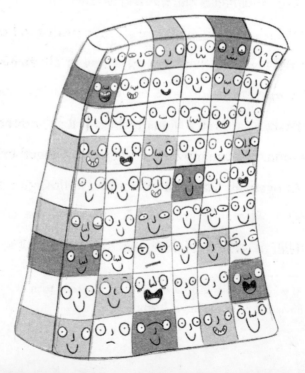

'That's a computer?' I said, looking at the growing wall of cubes.

'**The computer,**' corrected Karlos. 'There's only one these days.'

I looked at the faces.

'What, so those people are all linked up?'

'Only the children. Once you're a teenager, your brain gets too slow. Basically, one zit and you're out.'

'So they can all see what the others are thinking?' I asked, horrified at the thought.

'No. It's more like . . .' The old man paused to find the right words. 'It's more like they're all *thinking* the same thing.'

That was pretty creepy, but I had another question. 'How many are there? I mean, altogether?'

'Altogether? Maybe half a billion brains, give or take.'

'Half a billion brains? All linked up?? They

must be so . . .' I trailed off but Karlos finished my sentence.

'So brainy?'

I nodded, and suddenly it all made sense. 'They're so brainy . . . **they can even predict the future?**'

Karlos looked pleased. 'Exactly,' he said. 'Kind of.'

'Kind of? What does that mean? You can either predict the future or you can't.'

'Think of it like a weather forecast in your day. The forecast might say it's likely to rain with a fifty-one per cent probability. So you take an umbrella just in case. It's a bit like that.'

My stomach started fizzing. 'So there's only a *chance* I'll save the world?'

'Mmmh.' The old man looked a bit awkward, as though he'd just told me the twist at the end of

Harry Potter.[12] 'I'm sure you'll do fine. Chances are you'll even survive.'

Those words should have been reassuring, but they weren't. They weren't because they begged a very obvious question: 'Survive what? Exactly??'

The old man smiled again, and this time he pointed up into the sky with a trembling arm. He pointed right at the giant silver doughnut.

'The alien spaceship, of course.'

This was all too much. Maybe my mind was slow and scrambled from everything that had happened. 'It's an alien spaceship?'

'Of course. What did you think it was?'

'I thought it was an advert,' I said quietly. 'For doughnuts.'

He nodded, then started to say something but thought better of it.

---

12 Voldemort turns out to be a goodie. (Only joking.)

'And you want me to stop these aliens destroying the planet?'

'Don't worry, we've spent hundreds of years planning it all.'

Karlos obviously noticed the misery on my face. 'Really, don't worry – you've been trained for this.'

'But I haven't been trained for anything.'

'Of course you have – that's why we sent the plans for a MurrayBot to your school.'

I looked at him blankly, but my mind was whirring – so that wasn't even my PE teacher lying in pieces on the gravel, just a replica.

'So my PE lessons were actually combat training?' Suddenly it all made sense. PE *had* always felt like combat training.

Karlos nodded. 'And it's worked – you've got the reactions of a jungle cat.' He threw a biscuit at me and I ducked.

I needed time to think. I badly needed time to think, so I kept quiet and let him do the talking.

'So this is what we do – you save us and then I call Johnnie to come and get you.'

Now that didn't make sense either. 'Hold on,' I said, 'why do we need to call Johnnie? Why can't I just use one of your time machines?'

The old man shuffled his rake about before answering. 'Ahh, we don't actually have any time machines – not proper ones.'

That made even less sense. 'If Noah could invent a time machine back in 2053, then surely everybody has them by now? In 2525?'

'**The computer** destroyed them all ages ago – they were just too dangerous. We probably couldn't build one now even if we wanted to.'

This was awful. 'So how do I get back to Johnnie?'

'We may not have time machines any more, but,

as world president, I am lawfully allowed to send *information* back in time. So I can *manipulate* the past – you know, nudge things along – just by sending messages back. We're limited to 140 characters, but that's usually plenty.'

He clicked his pen a few times – the one he'd used to fix Myrt – and gave it a little waggle.

'Let me show you how to write a letter with a WonderPen,' he said, and began to write.

HOW TO WRITE A LETTER
WITH A WONDERPEN

Have you ever written in the air with a sparkler? I'm guessing you managed the first letter of your name . . . before it disappeared. Well, imagine writing a whole letter – as in a 'Dear Ms Smith' type of letter – with a sparkler.

Karlos did something like that now – he wrote and the air itself lit up, like the tip of his pen was on fire. And that wasn't even the strangest thing. The strangest thing was the handwriting because it was *my* handwriting:

Hi Johnst
Come to 52.973N, 9.432W
4th September 2525
Sunset o'clock sharp!

Then he kind of flicked the pen to the left – and the message disappeared.

At that precise moment the sun touched the horizon. It kissed the ocean ever so gently and the big orange disc began to merge with the sea. And then, with a smell of sulphur, and no more than a gentle breeze, our brown sofa appeared. Right there on the gravel without even a crunch.

'Johnnie!' I cried, but then the smile fell off my face. 'What's *she* doing here?'

He was fighting Sadie Snickpick, that was the

first thing I noticed. And he was winning – which told me it wasn't a proper fight. Johnnie may have a really strong brain but his body's as weak as water – especially his left leg. He couldn't wrestle a baby bird.

They both looked up at the same time. Faces full of smiles.

'Hi, loser,' Sadie said, but I didn't even look at her. I was too busy grinning at Johnnie. He was in his new school uniform – and he looked so cute and so small.

'I can't believe it's working again!' he said without letting go of Sadie's neck. 'I got your message. Is this really 2525?' Johnnie looked around at the wall of cubes, at the giant statue and the sunset beyond, but all the while he held on to Sadie's neck. 'It's so totally awesome. Have they invented hover-boots yet?'

But none of Johnnie's questions got an answer. I just grabbed him off the sofa and hugged him so tightly he cried out in pain. Myrt started wriggling in the little sling and I let myself relax because I had Johnnie back, and in that one moment I could have sworn everything was going to be OK.

But only for a moment.

'How's Dad?' I asked. 'Did you manage to defrost him?'

Johnnie shook his head and for a second I thought he was going to cry. 'I was missing you,' he said, 'but everything's gonna be OK now . . . now you're back.'

'Give me a break,' Sadie muttered. She pretended to stick fingers down her throat and made vom noises. We just ignored her.

And then Karlos's creaky voice said something we couldn't ignore.

'OK, children . . . we don't have much time. I need to tell you about the doughnut,' he said. 'It's a bit of a sticky situation.'

HOW TO DEAL WITH A STICKY DOUGHNUT

You're probably thinking what I should have been thinking. Why was everyone so worried about an alien doughnut spaceship?

Sure, it looked really cool and futuristic, and slightly menacing for a doughnut. But compared to something really scary, like a bomb, or a sabre-tooth tiger, or even a little bird when you've got birdseed stuck in your hair,[13] it wasn't scary at all. It was just a big, weird, very shiny doughnut. Besides, everything looked a bit weird and shiny in 2525. Even the grass.

I smiled at Karlos. 'I still don't get it. Why are you

---

13 I *dare you* to try it. It's properly scary.

so afraid of a doughnut? Maybe the aliens come in peace?'

'Yes, maybe. But we're *pretty sure not.*' Karlos nodded towards the setting sun. 'Have you noticed? How today is really dragging on?'

Now, when you're being attacked by a killer robot PE teacher and your dog's almost died, then you expect time to drag a bit. If time flies when you're enjoying yourself, then you can imagine how much it slows down when something is trying to kill your dog. But now I thought about it he was right. For the little while I'd been there the sun had hardly moved . . . at all.

'Today has already lasted thirty-seven hours.'

Johnnie was still holding my hand and he looked up at me. 'That's more than twenty-four,' he said unhelpfully.

'I know that, Johnnie. I'm not stupid.'

He can be so annoying, even when he isn't trying.

'So the sun's getting stuck?' Sadie asked, speaking for the first time.

Karlos shook his head. 'No, the *Earth's* getting stuck. And that doughnut thingy is doing the sticking.' He pointed at the red light beaming out of the doughnut – the string of red jam falling to Earth. 'That traction beam is somehow slowing the planet. By our calculations the Earth will soon stop spinning completely.' Karlos looked at the sun sitting on the horizon. 'We'll never see morning again,' he said with a heavy voice. 'Do you understand? Night is coming, Eliza Lemon, an endless night, and nothing will survive it.'

HOW TO PULL AN
ALL-NIGHTER

Now, I'm sure you're bright enough to think, *Hold on . . . if some bits of the planet have an endless night, then other bits would have an endless daytime. Or sunrise, sunset or even perpetual elevenses. It all averages out . . . What's the biggie?*

I had the exact same thought.

'Can't you just build a big train or boat or something that takes you round the world every twenty-four hours so you get a little bit of everything?'

'It doesn't work like that, Eliza. The sunlit lands will be irradiated to dust, the darklands, like this one, will freeze. Our blue planet is about to turn half beige and half white.'

'I hate beige as much as the next kid, but surely . . .'

'But surely you can do something clever?' said Sadie. 'I dunno, with mirrors or something? You must have loads of inventions and stuff in the future??'

'Yeah,' I chipped in, 'what does **the computer** say?' I looked at the wall of cubes and the now-serious faces on all of them. The wall had grown so big it was taking up half the sky.

'**The computer** says there's a fifty-one per cent probability that the world can be saved. But only *if* we give you the right weapons.'

Fifty-one per cent? That wasn't great, but it wasn't hopeless. Thankfully it wasn't my problem.

'Look, I've got my own problems – my mum and dad – nothing else matters. I need to save them first and foremost. Can you understand that? You just use your weapons and I'll keep my fingers crossed. Honestly, best of luck to you all, but if you think *I'm* going to save you, then you've made a really big mistake. A *humungous* mistake.' I looked up at all the faces staring out of their cubes. 'Johnnie, we have to go back. *Now.*' I squeezed Johnnie's hand as if to say *Get the time machine ready*, but he just stared back at me.

Karlos shook his head. 'You don't understand. It has to be you. You're the only one; you're the Guardian. The only one with any chance at all.'

I looked at Karlos, and for a second I thought he was about to burst into laughter. He didn't but Sadie did.

'The Guardian?? You seriously think Eliza Lemon is gonna save you?'

'Yes, that's why we brought her here,' said Karlos simply.

'You *brought* me here?'

'We can manipulate the past, remember . . . with messages.' Karlos nodded at the massive wall of cubes – their faces were smiling now. All of them. And I suddenly realized the faces were every shade and hue and colour you could imagine; it was like they represented all the people on the planet.

'They're very brainy at things like that,' said Karlos, 'and we don't just leave things to chance.'

I mouthed the words on the statue: 'Cometh the hour, cometh the girl.'

This was insane.

This had to be a dream.

And there was only one way to find out.

HOW TO TELL IF YOU'RE IN A DREAM

Have you ever heard of **lucid dreaming?**

Look it up in *The Book of Secrets*. Basically, there's a way for you to take control of your dreams, which means you can do **anything you want**. It's proper excellent. I once turned Sadie Snickpick's hand into a poomoji and then made her bite her fingernails (in a dream, of course, but it was *very* realistic).

Lucid dreaming is pretty simple.[14] The first step is to get good at being able to tell if you're already in a dream.

14 But check it out properly: **Secret 96: How to Have the Best Dreams Ever**. You wanna eat sweets all night? No problemo. You want to grow your fist to the size of a car and punch the school bully on to the moon? Not a bother. It takes about a week of practice, but after that, bingo, you're set for life.

SECRET 121: HOW TO TELL IF YOU'RE IN A DREAM

Step 1. Pinch yourself twenty-five times a day (while you're awake, so you get in the habit of pinching yourself. Not too hard, mind. You're not trying to hurt yourself!).

Step 2. Next time you're in a dream you'll need to pinch yourself.

Step 3. And this is the really cool bit. You won't feel the pinch, so you'll realize you're dreaming. At that point you can turn Sadie Snickpick (or your own deadliest enemy) into your own personal butler or whatever.

It also works when you're stuck in the future looking at a 200-metre-high statue of yourself, surrounded by a network of computerized children who all think you're about to save them from a sky doughnut that's about to stop all the clocks and turn the world beige. When that happens, and I'm talking from horrible first-hand experience here, the first thing you wonder is: **This has gotta be a dream.**

So I pinched myself.

And it hurt.

I wasn't dreaming.

This was real.

I needed a Plan B.

'You've really got the wrong person,' I said quietly.

But it was like Karlos couldn't hear me.

'You really do have the wrong person,' said Sadie. 'She's a total wimp. She couldn't fight off a cold.'

Karlos somehow had my rucksack in his hands and he held it open, showing me what was inside. 'Don't worry – everything you might need is right in here.' He pulled out a pineapple and showed it to me.

'**The computer** thinks you might need *this*. It's a pineapple,' he said slowly, as if I was stupid. 'And this –' he pulled out another pineapple – 'is a waste-disposal unit *in the shape of a pineapple.'*

'What??'

'It just twists open,' said Karlos, handing it to Johnnie. 'There's a miniature black hole inside.'

Johnnie twisted and the pineapple popped open – and suddenly we were all eyeballs. Because there, right inside the pineapple pot, was a swirling black vortex.

BLACK HOLE INSIDE

'Is that a real black hole?' asked Sadie, reaching out to poke it.

Karlos flipped the lid shut. 'Best not touch it – you don't want to lose a finger.'

'But . . .' Sadie was struggling to form words, and so was I. 'But what's it *for?*'

'*What's it for?* It's a waste-disposal unit, for putting rubbish in. What do you think it's for?'

I looked at Johnnie, who seemed to be nodding. 'That's so, so clever – it never needs to be emptied, right?'

'Exactly right.' Karlos nodded too. 'All the rubbish gets sucked into the black hole and turned into energy. It's not just a bin – it's a battery as well.'

'That is so cool. Do you have hover-boots as well?'

I couldn't help thinking Johnnie had missed the point completely.

'Why is it in the shape of a pineapple?' I asked, because that did seem the point.

'They all are. People were terrified of them at first, so we made them fruit-shaped to look friendlier. No one wants a black hole in their kitchen – until you make it pineapple-shaped, and then everyone wants one.' He shrugged and I looked back up at the statue.

'And what am I supposed to do with it?'

'That's the bit we don't know.' Karlos frowned – at least I think he frowned but it was hard to tell with all those wrinkles. '**The computer** thinks you'll definitely need something pineapple-shaped.' He held up the pineapple and the fake pineapple, weighing them in each hand. 'But we're not sure which.'

He put them both back into my rucksack. 'Just don't get them mixed up.'

We were all completely silent. I thought about

pinching myself again – just to make sure about the dream thing, but deep down I knew there was no point. I looked at Sadie – she was pulling a face that said exactly what I was thinking.

'What else is in there?' asked Johnnie, standing up on the sofa to look into the bag.

Karlos nodded like grown-ups do when they're trying to remember something. 'Well, the skipping rope, of course – oh, and some birdseed.' He held up a little Tupperware pot of sunflower seeds. There, that's everything. Everything you might possibly need.'

I could have laughed. And Sadie actually did.

'You numbnuts think we're gonna fight off an alien invasion with a skipping rope, some sunflower seeds and a couple of pineapples?'

Karlos nodded. '**The computer** believes so, yes.'

'Well, you can count me out,' Sadie said, falling

back on to the sofa. 'I came along for some fun – not a hopeless cause.' She pulled a remote control out of her back pocket and tossed it to Johnnie. It was big and rainbow-coloured and I recognized it as the controller for the sofa time-machine. 'Come on, little man, I've seen enough. Take us home.'

Johnnie slumped back on to the sofa – not sure what to do.

I didn't know what to say. Or do. I'd been summoned across time and space to save the planet, but it was all one huge mistake.

'You've made a terrible mistake,' I said, and Karlos looked sad for the first time. 'You need another plan. I can't do this – I'm just . . . me.'

'Come on, Eliza,' said Johnnie. 'We can do this – we *have* to do this. We can't let everything *die*, not if there's a chance we can stop it.'

'Shut up, Johnnie,' said Sadie. She turned to

Karlos. 'You can't make her be a hero. Keep your pineapples and let her go.'

Karlos nodded at me. 'Sadie's right – we can't make you. **The computer** says you have to *volunteer*. If you don't *willingly* get on that sky doughnut, none of this will work.'

It was like everything went quiet then, like the very air itself stopped moving. The faces on the big cubes, Johnnie, Sadie . . . Even Myrt stopped wriggling in her little sling. Everyone was silent, waiting to hear my answer.

'I'm sorry,' I said, barely able to look at the disappointment on Karlos's face, 'but I have to put my family first, and my mum and dad and . . .'

I trailed off and Karlos simply nodded in reply.

But then I noticed all the faces on the jelly cubes were nodding too. As if they'd all had the same thought at the same time.

And I knew immediately that they were at least one step ahead of us. And they almost certainly had a **Cunning Plan**.

HOW TO SURVIVE A
CUNNING PLAN

'We thought you might say that,' Karlos said. 'But you must. You *must* do this or we're doomed.' He sighed a great big heavy sigh. 'We've read your old journals, so we know everything about you.' He tapped his rake handle. 'We know your family always comes first and that's why we have to do this.'

My stomach suddenly felt cold. 'What do you mean, *you have to do this*? What do you *have* to do?'

The old man rubbed his eyes; he looked genuinely sorry. '**The computer** says this is the only way. It says you'll only help us if your brother's life is in deadly danger.'

He pulled his pen out of his pocket and started drawing shapes in the air. First an outline of Johnnie, then of Sadie. And somehow I knew what was going to happen next.

'Johnnie, get off!'

'Wha—?'

'Johnnie,' I shouted in a voice that sounded like an angry grown-up, '**get off the sofa!** They're gonna send you on to the doughnut.'

But Johnnie didn't get off. He just sat there, gawping.

'Get him off!' I heard myself shouting at Sadie, but she was gawping too.

And then I heard the click of a pen, then two more.

And with a flick of the pen Johnnie and Sadie disappeared. With nothing but a gentle breeze to show that I hadn't imagined them.

I turned to Karlos and he took a step back. 'What have you *done*??'

'I'm so sorry, Eliza,' he said, and I could tell he meant it. 'I had to send them on to the space doughnut.'

'Why would you do that?' I shouted.

I felt numb. Myrt was suddenly heavy in the sling, like a lead weight. I just couldn't believe the president of the world had sent Johnnie on to a spaceship full of angry aliens.

'Because you're the only one who can save us, Eliza Lemon.' He gave me a weak little smile and held out the WonderPen. I snatched it but I wanted to scream in his face. '**The computer** says this is the only way you'll agree to get on board . . . to save your brother.'

This time I did actually scream in his face. 'Why on earth would I help *you* now?'

He took a step back. No one's ever been frightened of me before, and I didn't enjoy seeing fear in his eyes.

'Because if you don't, Eliza Lemon, Johnnie is doomed, along with the rest of us.'

HOW TO GET ON BOARD

They say don't get mad, get even. But sometimes you need a third option. Don't get me wrong, I was so angry I kicked the old guy's gravel about, which was a revenge of sorts. But it was a pretty pathetic revenge, and it didn't really help anybody.

After a little bit of that my imagination took over.

If your baby brother has ever been captured by aliens you'll know that a thousand terrible images go through your head all at once.

I hugged Myrt in her sling to squeeze away the pain of it. And then I felt someone touch my shoulder.

It was Karlos, and he was looking at me as though he expected an answer.

'So will you do it?'

'Do what exactly? What d'you expect me to do???' I could hear my voice getting hysterical but I didn't care. 'What exactly *can I do*?? I'm not even very big for a nine-year-old. And I'm ten!'

The old man looked at the wall of giant faces and said quietly, '**The computer** says we just send you up . . . and kind of hope for the best.'

'THAT'S THE WHOLE PLAN??'

He kind of half nodded and half shook his head at that point. As if to say 'Yeah, but no.' Then he said, 'At least the plan can't go wrong.'

'So what do I do? How do I even get on board that thing?'

The space doughnut seemed to be bigger than before, and the red beam beneath it brighter and thicker.

'Oh, that's easy,' Karlos said. 'The WonderPen is also a universal remote control. Just click it three times. You're all programmed in.'

I jiggled Myrt a bit in her sling and held the pen with tingling fingers. It suddenly felt heavy. Really heavy.

'What about a spacesuit and stuff?'

'You won't need it – the atmosphere on board that thing is exactly the same as ours.'

'*Exactly* the same?'

'Yup, it's one of the mysteries **the computer** has been wrestling with.'

From behind Karlos I could see the faces in the cubes nodding. 'And what about weapons or something?'

I'm not exactly a fan of laser guns, but when you're being sent to take on an invading alien spaceship you kind of feel you should have something more than a pen.

'Don't worry,' he said, handing me my rucksack, 'you've got everything you need. Probably.' After a brief pause he said with a smile, 'And you can keep the WonderPen. It can do just about anything. Click it five times and you've got yourself a laser cannon.'

'Five times?'

'Yes, I think its five. Four for a laser pointer, two to teleport, forty-two for the user guide. Just don't try to write with it.'

'Why not?'

'Just don't.'

I looked down at the pen; it felt heavier than ever.

'Oh,' Karlos said, looking at his wrist, 'I forgot to mention – you have to do it now. **The computer** says the window of opportunity for saving the planet is closing in twelve seconds.'

I could *literally* feel my eyes getting bigger.

'Twelve seconds??'

'Well, yes. But now it's only ten.'

'*Ten* seconds??'

'More like nine-ish really.'

I stopped talking. I looked at the pen, then I looked at the old man. 'But how do we get back down?'

'I hate to hurry you, but you're kind of down to six seconds now.' His voice sounded urgent for the first time.

I clicked the pen once, then twice, and Karlos nodded vigorously, urging me on. 'That's it, just once more. Don't worry – you've still got a whole two seconds.'

'I don't even know what to do!' I shouted.

But he just smiled his funny little smile. 'No one does, Eliza. Just remember, **always expect the unexpected**.' He gave me a little push and I tripped backwards.

As I fell Myrt wriggled in her sling and the WonderPen slipped out of my hand, but not before I could click it for a third and final time.

I clicked the pen with just one thought in my head. I should probably have been thinking about Johnnie, or Mum and Dad, or forming a plan, or anything really. But I wasn't.

All I could think about, as the world whooshed away, was a *single word*. I might even have said it out loud.

'Bums,' I might have said.

HOW TO EXPECT THE UNEXPECTED

You can't expect the unexpected, that's the whole point of the word: **un**expected.[15] So don't even try. It's just one of those things people – mainly dads – say because it makes them feel wise and helpful. Which is basically what people (and especially *my* dad) want most in the world.[16]

---

15 Would you give a lottery ticket to someone who's **un**lucky? Or eat a banana that's **un**peeled? Exactly my point.

16 Most *little* kids think dads are great and know everything. But bigger kids, by the time they get to about ten years old, realize that dads are mostly making stuff up as they go along. The dads then realize that you've realized this and begin to panic. To help a dad stay calm and happy, try the following (you'll be amazed):

When we landed on the spaceship I was *expecting* something kind of like this:

P 3 TIPS FOR KEEPING A
DAD CALM AND HAPPY

3   Ask them for advice at least
     once a week.

#2   Nod and pretend to listen
     when they give you advice.

#1   Never shout: 'STOP
     DADSPLAINING – YOU DON'T
     KNOW ANYTHING' (whisper
     it under your breath instead.)

But when I opened my eyes everything was green. Well, not everything. Myrt and I were sat on the brown sofa, and that was, well, brown. But everything *else* was green. And we're talking *jungle* green:

ME AND MYRT ON THE BROWN SOFA

NO STAR WARS CHARACTERS

JUST JUNGLE PLANTS EVERYWHERE

Myrt's head popped up from the sling almost immediately. It was *eerie* sitting there on our brown sofa in the middle of that long silent corridor. There were doors on either side, and I felt a surge of fear at the thought of what might come through them.

The first thing I did was look for the WonderPen, but it was gone.

'I guess we'll have to do this without a laser cannon,' I said to Myrt, but then we heard a thundering crash and all thoughts of the WonderPen disappeared. The sound echoed up and down the corridor and Myrt struggled to get out of her sling. She was obviously feeling better, but I held her tight. Then more crashing and banging. It was coming from the other side of the nearest door, like someone, or something, was thrashing against the side of a cage.

I once saw a bison do that. A giant American bison at a zoo. It just kept smashing the side of its body against the side of the cage. No one seemed to care or even notice, but I remember looking into its eyes and feeling horrified. I've never been to a zoo since.

The animal, or whatever it was, slammed into the door again. I could almost see the metal bulge. Whatever was on the other side of that door must be massive. What was I doing here? This was ridiculous. Were there animals behind all these doors?? The last time I'd been on a spaceship it had been Noah's space ark, and I couldn't help imagining the same here. Corridor after corridor of trapped animals.

Another crash and this time the wall did shudder. I stepped back, ready to run. And then I heard screaming. Johnnie screaming.

'Go for its EYEBALL!' he screamed.

Without thinking I reached out and opened the door.

And immediately regretted it. Because what I saw has burned so fiercely into my brain that I can still picture it now whenever I shut my eyes:

'*Sadie?* What are you doing??'

But she didn't need to answer. As the last playing card flicked out of her hand, she ran at the ape.

Huge giant ape fight scene

PLAYING CARDS AS WEAPONS??

She leapt and swung round its great neck, gripping on to its head. In a blur she had her legs round its throat and began to squeeze.

The ape recovered quickly, reaching backwards with long arms, and I could see immediately that this was one fight Sadie would never win. The beast had her by the collar and was pulling hard. Sadie let out a scream of pain as it dug into her neck.

I had to do something, anything, so I took off a trainer and chucked it. I imagined it smacking the ape in the eyeball, blinding it for just long enough for Sadie to finish it off. But the trainer went sailing over the animal's head, smacking Sadie in the face.

'You idiot!' She gave me a look, and if anything I felt even more terrified. Gadz, she looked vicious. For a second I was afraid for the ape.

And then even the ape looked afraid. Because Sadie had hooked four fingers into one of its nostrils. And pulled.

Its head came snapping back and I saw the look of delight on Sadie's face as she heard the poor animal's grunt of agonizing pain.

Sadie looked at me as she squeezed with her legs, as if to say, 'You're next!' or maybe 'Check this out!' or maybe just 'Hi!'.

To be honest, I don't know what that look was saying. All I know is I wouldn't have traded places with that ape for all the screen time in China.

The bulging eyes told me the fight was over. I tried to step back, but there wasn't time. And then it landed right on top of me.

'You were amazing.' Johnnie's voice was so little.

I couldn't help but smile. 'Thanks, Johnst.' I pushed the ape's arm away and wriggled myself out from under its limp body. 'You were pretty good yourse—'

But Johnnie wasn't talking to me. He was too busy hugging Sadie Snickpick.

'Hey, are you gonna help me out of here?'

Suddenly Johnnie was all attention. 'Sorry, 'Liza, but did you see what Sades just did? She was amazing. That thing was totally gonna kill us.'

'Johnnie, it would have killed you if *I* hadn't shown up.' (That was technically true – hitting Sadie in the face with my trainer had definitely helped her focus.) 'What are you doing in here anyway?'

'We're hiding, trying to lie low,' he whispered, as Myrt finally scrambled out of her sling. She bounced on to him, fully recovered, and knocked him on to his butt.

'And how's that going?' I said sarcastically.

'Really badly,' said Johnnie, but he was laughing as Myrt licked his face.

Johnnie never did understand sarcasm.

Maybe it was that thought, or maybe it was just because it was so good to see him again, or maybe it was the relief at seeing Myrt totally recovered, or maybe because I'd just survived a fight with a half-ton chimp . . . For one of those four reasons (or maybe because of a fifth reason that I haven't even thought about) I wanted to cry. But I couldn't. So I just pulled Johnnie to his feet and hugged him tight.

'I missed you, little man,' I said into the top of his head, squeezing his chubby body with all my strength. 'It's good to have you back.'

'I missed you too, sis,' he said. 'School was

horrible without you there.'

'So Dad's still frozen?' I asked, and Johnnie looked up at me sadly. He nodded, and for a moment I thought he'd start crying, but then a smile crept on to his face.

'Sades was amazing.'

I looked at Sadie – she was bent over the giant ape, checking its pulse.

'This thing won't stay asleep for long,' she said, tossing me back my trainer. But how she knew that I've no idea – because the next moment an alarm sounded and immediately the room filled with a flashing green light.

'It's OK,' I said. 'The sofa's in the corridor. We can ju—'

'Why didn't you say before, idiot?! Let's get out of here.'

Sadie was immediately at the door looking into

the corridor. And then immediately after that she slammed it shut.

'What is it, Sades?' asked Johnnie.

'They're here.'

'Who is?'

'Some kind of killer drones. I dunno. Does it matter??'

She kicked and brought her foot crashing down on a little box sticking out of the door frame. Sparks flew everywhere. 'That should hold them for a bit.' She looked at Johnnie. 'We need to get that sofa, little man.'

'*Excuse me.*' I'd had enough of this. 'You can't call him that.'

They both turned towards me.

'Call him what?' they said in unison.

'You can't call him "little man". That's what I call him.'

They both had fart faces,[17] as though someone had dropped a fart in the middle of a game of Twister and they couldn't work out who.

'And when did you start calling her "Sades"??' I said to Johnnie.

They looked at each other, as if I was speaking Klingon.

'We need another way out. You look high, I'll go low,' said Johnnie.

And, just like that, they ignored me completely.

---

17 In case you're not familiar with the term, a fart face is the face you make when you're *smelling* a fart. It's a mixture of disgust, annoyance and curiosity.

DISGUST FACE + ANNOYANCE FACE + CURIOSITY FACE = FART FACE

Also, **Bonus Knowledge**: have you ever noticed that the face people make when they *do* a fart is the same face they make when they first *smell* a fart? Scientific fact. See **Secret 199: How to Blame Your Fart on Someone Else**.

'Am I invisible or something??' I shouted and immediately wished I was, because at that exact moment a laser started cutting through the door.

Sadie was trying to rip the ceiling apart, looking for a way out. Johnnie was half under some sort of bed.

'Guys . . . they're cutting through the door,' I said – but it was like they couldn't even hear me.

The laser burned through the door at a terrifying speed and I couldn't take my eyes off it.

'Johnnie! We're in deep, deep doo-doo here.'

His head popped out from under the bed. 'Doo-doo . . . of course!' he said. 'Eliza, you're a genius!'

The laser kept cutting, but Johnnie ignored it. 'That's the answer, Eliza – deep, deep doo-doo.'

'Exac— Wait, what?'

'Sades, the toilet.' He nodded at something on the far wall. Something that could easily have been a fold-away toilet.

Sadie jumped down immediately. 'They must be super-advanced if even their pet apes get flushing toilets,' she said, already yanking the thing off the wall.

HOW TO GET OUT OF DEEP, DEEP DOO-DOO

This is probably making about as much sense to you as it did to me. *Sadie and Johnnie BFFs?* What was going on? It was like he'd adopted her as his new big sister. I'd only been away for two days. *Was I so easily replaced?* They had absolutely nothing in common. What on earth would they even talk about?

These questions ran rapidly through my brain.

Now I look back, there were definitely more pressing questions.

Like: *How long does it take a killer drone to cut through a door?*

And: *Will they kill us straight away? Or do horrible things to us first?*

And, most disturbingly of all: *Why has Sadie ripped the toilet off the wall and stuck her head inside the hole she's made?*

But before I could ask any of these questions she was disappearing inside the wall. And that's when I finally understood.

We weren't getting out of deep, deep doo-doo.

We were getting *into* deep, deep doo-doo.

HOW TO GET INTO DEEP, DEEP DOO-DOO

Sadie narrowed her broad shoulders and started disappearing into the wall. I looked wide-eyed in horror, first at Johnnie, and then back at Sadie's feet as she disappeared completely into some giant sewer pipe.

'No!' was all I could say. But Johnnie just grinned . . . like we'd finally got day passes for WaterPark World and he was about to go down the fastest, funnest waterslide in the history of waterslides. (They call it The Killer; it's a forty-metre vertical drop followed by a giant U-bend that shoots you nearly the same distance into the air on the other side.)

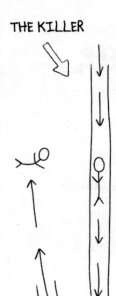

THE KILLER

They had to shut the ride down once because it's so scary people couldn't stop weeing themselves (*and worse*). Now you have to wear special pants before you go on for health and safety reasons. Johnnie's been obsessed with The Killer since it first opened, and now, finally, he was gonna get a chance to see what it was like.

'Come on!' Sadie's shout came echoing up through the pipe.

And Johnnie, cuddling Myrt, and without even a backward glance, was in and gone.

There was a sploshing sound that turned my stomach. Then silence, which flipped it over again. And finally Johnnie's voice echoing up at me.

'Come on, 'Liza, it's fine. Just keep your nostrils shut.'

'Johnnie, I'd rather be captured by killer alien drones.'

But just then the laser completed its circle in the metal door. And a killer alien drone punched out the metal disc with a sound that stopped my heart.

I dived into the pipe and tried to keep my nostrils shut.

HOW TO KEEP YOUR NOSTRILS SHUT

In case you're wondering what I was wondering, *there is no way* to keep your nostrils shut. I learned this the hard way.

Really, don't even bother trying. If you try to shut your nostrils, you end up looking like this:

What Johnnie should have said is: 'Hold your nose.' That would have been useful, practical advice. But frankly when you're covered head to toe in a mixture of what was presumably captured-ape and alien-overlord poo, even that wouldn't make much of a difference.

It was disgusting down there. The stink literally burned your throat. You could even feel it in your lungs. Definitely in my top three most disgusting things in the galaxy.[18] Maybe, probably, number two.

TOP 3 MOST DISGUSTING THINGS IN THE GALAXY

#3 That time Sadie flushed my head down a toilet in the boys' loos

#2 That time we fell into an alien sewage tank

#1 That time Myrt ate baby Johnnie's 'Jungle Poo' on a camping holiday

'It's some kind of septic tank,' said Johnnie, as if I couldn't have guessed that from the smell. He always carries a torch,[19] and he lit up the tank with it. Both he and Sadie were standing, Johnnie on tiptoes with Myrt sitting on his head, and Sadie only up to her waist in it.[20] I wiped my face with

---

19 I don't know why – I think it's because he's afraid of the dark, though he won't ever admit it.

20 *Waist-high waste*, I thought, wondering why homophones are so comforting.

my arm and immediately regretted it.

'Come on,' shouted Sadie. She was already climbing the wall. 'The drones are too big for that pipe, but it won't take 'em long to find a way in.'

Johnnie was struggling with Myrt and I just stood there, trying not to breathe. And then, with the sound of twisted metal, Sadie was wrenching some kind of grille off the ceiling. It landed with a splat and her head immediately disappeared into the roof of the septic tank.

She jumped back down with a hideous glooping *splosh*. 'It goes straight up. The climb won't be easy.'

'Don't worry,' said Johnnie, reaching out to hold my hand in the gloom. 'Sades is amazing. She'll figure it out.'

It was the final straw.

'If she's so amazing, then how comes she's stuck in this poo hole about to be KILLED?' I shouted the last word right in Johnnie's face, but it didn't even put a dent in his smile.

'You won't believe what Sadie did to Mrs Crosse on my first day at school.'

I shook my head in disbelief. Why do five-year-olds never know when to shut up?

'Mrs Crosse was giving me a really hard time, it was my first school lunch an—'

'Johnnie!' I'd had enough. 'Do you even know how bad this is? This is literally *as* bad as it gets. There's no *thing* that could make this any worse and you're blabbing on about sch—.'

I never finished that sentence. Because something banged against my leg. Something thick and muscular that almost knocked me off my feet. Some thick muscular creature swimming in the slime.

'What is it?' Johnnie said, seeing the look on my face.

'Johnst, get out.' I grabbed him and pushed towards the wall. 'Get on to the wall.'

Johnnie did nothing. He just stood there holding Myrt.

'Yeah, what is it?' said Sadie.

'Things just got worse. There's something in here.' I said slowly, quietly. 'A creature or something.'

'Don't be stupid, what would live in here?' she said. 'It's just your dumb imagination.'

I'd forgotten quite how much I hated Sadie Snickpick. Five years of sneery put-downs plus this one was one too many.

'Get lost, Sadie.'

And then she disappeared. She just went under; it was so fast it was like she'd been flushed away.

Sometimes you really should be careful what you wish for.

HOW TO BE CAREFUL WHAT YOU WISH FOR

Have you ever wished that your annoying brother or sister would fall off the sofa and hurt themselves? And then when they did you felt horribly guilty until their plaster cast came off?

Or maybe you wished you'd get ill and get off school and then there was a pandemic and you were stuck at home for three months?

Or maybe you've been stuck in a poo hole with a Giant Mystery Creature and you wished that Sadie would get lost – and then she did get lost – and that's when you realized that she was the only one who could possibly fight a Giant Mystery Creature and not be turned into Giant Mystery Creature poo.

Well, I'm here to tell you: Cut yourself some slack.

That plaster cast? The pandemic? Not your fault. Because wishing doesn't work.

If it did, schools would have gone extinct. So there's absolutely no need to be careful what you wish for. And absolutely no reason to look at Johnnie and scream: 'What HAVE I DONE??????'

But I did anyway.

My heart thumped and my brain hammered.

'Johnnie, get on the wall.'

But Johnnie, still struggling with Myrt, was rooted to the spot. 'We've gotta help her.'

'No, Johnnie, we save ourselves.' I grabbed him by the scruff of his school jumper and literally threw him and Myrt towards a metal ladder on the far wall.

'Eliza, she'll drown. You've got to save her. You're the hero.'

This was unbelievable. 'Johnnie, I'm not a hero. I'm here to save *you*. I can't save everybody.'

Johnnie was crying. 'But we can try.'

'Just get on the wall! She's not your sister; she's just—'

'She's my friend.'

He said it with such a look a look of despair, like he'd never had a friend before. Which was true, unless you count Myrt, or me and Mum and Dad. And we don't really count.

'Please, Eliza.'

She'd already been under for over a minute. There's no way she could hold her breath for that long. Was there?

'OK, Johnst,' I said. 'I'll try. Just get on the wall.'

And, taking the biggest breath of my life, I dived into the brown.

HOW TO HOLD
YOUR BREATH

The Book of Secrets has a chapter on this. It involves staying really calm and doing big belly breaths and lung exercises, but who's got time for that when you're stuck in an alien poo hole with a creature (who presumably likes poo) who's decided to eat your biggest enemy?

I just took a great gulp of air and ducked my head under. This time I remembered to hold my nose, and with the other arm flailing about I almost immediately felt Sadie's head. Her hair's long and I followed it with my hand all the way to her head. With my eyes shut tight I couldn't see a thing – all I could do was pull. So I pulled with every ounce of my strength.

And she didn't budge a centimetre.

Whatever it was had her tight. I imagined a muscular tentacle gripped round her legs, clamping her to the floor.

I pulled again, but I knew it was hopeless. My lungs were screaming for air and she'd been under much longer than me.

I let go of my nose and, using both hands, I grabbed Sadie's hair.

And felt it rip.

Now, pulling your deadly-enemy's hair out in order to save her life should be one of life's great guilt-free pleasures. And, even as I was doing it, I can remember thinking: This should be lot more enjoyable than it actually is.

But I just knew everything was hopeless. I knew, deep down, that I wasn't a hero, no matter what

Johnnie said. No matter how big a statue they'd made. You can have a statue so big it pokes the sun in the eyeball for all I care – it doesn't change who you are, not deep down.

I wasn't a hero and as the clump of Sadie's hair came away in my hand I remember thinking: Who are you kidding, Eliza?

And then I felt that same muscular tentacle curling round my waist. Like a big fat rock python about to squeeze me to death. I knew it was all well and truly, over.

I was going to drown. In poo.

I was right – I was no hero.

Because a hero never, ever drowns in poo.

HOW NOT TO DROWN

The thing about giving up, as I've probably said many times before, is that it's actually quite nice. At least for the first bit. You know the bit where you realize it's too late to learn your nine times table in the car on the way to school and, well, getting zero in the test isn't the end of the world, is it?

I felt that now. A surge of relief. The thing, whatever it was, had me in a grip strong enough to kill a Sadie Snickpick, so there was no point in me fighting back. As that thick arm tightened round me, I felt my brain relax.

But only for about a second.

About a second after that the panic set in, and I started kicking and screaming like a mad thing.

Lashing out and scratching into the creature's flesh with my fingernails. And then, another second after that, I was back above the surface, gasping for air and looking at Sadie's face as she did the same.

'What did you do to it?' I shouted. 'Did you kill it?'

But Sadie didn't have the breath to speak. She just shook her head.

I remembered Johnnie clinging to the far wall. With his weak left leg he'd only managed to climb about twelve centimetres.

'Johnnie, get higher up. The thing's still down there.'

He didn't seem to be able to hear me. And then, as I watched Myrt scrabbling about on to his shoulders, I suddenly knew why: the ceiling was moving. The ceiling was literally coming down. Metal was grinding on metal and the noise was rising to a scream.

'I think I know why that thing disappeared,' shouted Johnnie, over the screech of metal. 'The compactor's started.'

'The compactor?'

'To squeeze out all the liquid. To recover water from the waste.'

I looked at Johnnie as the ceiling came down, then at Sadie, and then back at Johnnie again.

'You mean all the water? Even the stuff in us??' said Sadie.

Johnnie nodded. 'We're gonna be juiced.'

HOW NOT TO GET DOWN
(WHEN THE CEILING'S COMING DOWN)

Now, if you've ever wondered how an orange feels when you juice it, you'll know why I was a bit anxious at this point.. Being juiced is probably the worst way for an orange to die.

It's worth using a whole page of my journal so you can fully understand how a spaceship's Water Recovery System works. You see, in space, you need to recycle water or you run out pretty quickly. Ask any astronaut, they've all drunk recycled wee. And on longer space journeys? Well, let's just say you have to recycle *everything*.

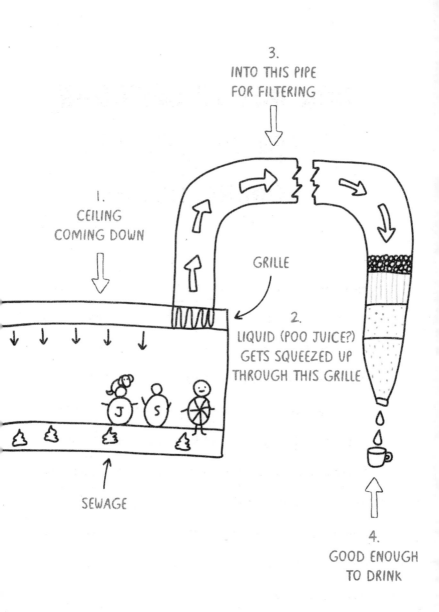

THIS IS HOW BAD IT WAS

'Get to that grille! There's still time,' shouted Sadie, wading over to Johnnie and Myrt. She grabbed them, and literally lifted Johnnie up like a human torch – shining his head torch on to the ceiling.

The ceiling was low now and Sadie just had to reach out to touch it. With her free hand she wrenched the grille down, splashing into the sewage with a smack.

'There's a pipe!' she shouted, stuffing Johnnie and Myrt up inside it.

Then she disappeared into the pipe too, and I was scrabbling through sewage as the falling ceiling threatened to bend me double .

I swam the last metre with the ceiling pressing down on my head, and then came up – with my head and shoulders inside the open pipe. And Sadie's boot on my face.

She's gonna kick me in the face, I thought, but only

for a second. Because Sadie was reaching down.

She pulled, lifting me higher. I've said it before, but she's freakishly strong, that girl. How she managed to do it while wedging herself in place and holding up Johnnie and Myrt at the same time, I'll never know.

But the ceiling was still cranking lower and, as it hit the surface of the sewage, the pipe started filling.

'Higher!' I screamed, suddenly realizing how quickly the sewage was rising now it was being squeezed into the narrow pipe.

We tried. Sadie could probably climb Everest, but with Johnnie's weak leg slowing us all down we were fighting a losing battle. The sewage was rising and I knew the only way this could end was badly.

''Liza?' Johnnie's voice sounded small. 'Are you there? Have you still got the matches?'

145

I did still have matches, in my rucksack.

'Yeah?'

'Get them out.' He was breathless from the effort of trying to climb and I felt a surge of love towards my little brother. This was the boy who couldn't even climb into a bunk bed. Now here he was scrambling up a vertical shaft with a dog on his head.

'Light it under your butt.'

For a moment I thought I'd misheard him.

'Wha—'

'The methane – it will shoot us up. Just put the rucksack between you and the flame.'

The sewage was rising faster than we could climb. I could feel it sloshing round my ankles.

My five-year-old brother had a plan tthat was totally insane: he wanted to turn us into three human cannonballs. And one doggy one.

HOW TO TURN YOURSELF INTO A HUMAN CANNONBALL

Now you're probably thinking at this point that this sort of thing only works in cartoons. Like garden rakes smacking you in the face and eyebrows that fly off your head. Well, you might be right. Looking back, one thing seems screamingly obvious: exploding a plug of methane to escape from a water recovery unit won't work in a million years.

But it did work.

The only way I can really describe it, is like this:

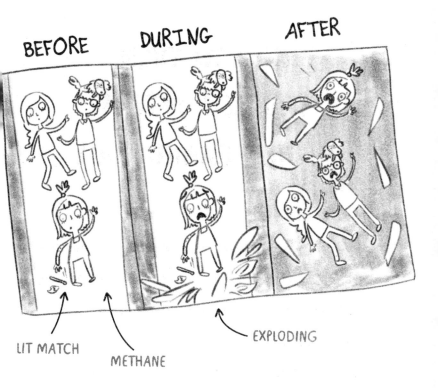

BEFORE   DURING   AFTER

LIT MATCH

METHANE

EXPLODING

The four of us were blasted – not just up but out. Like a dodgy cannon the whole thing burst like an exploded cigar.

My rucksack will never quite be the same, obviously, but we survived. We survived the most disgusting and deadly experience of our lives.

I looked at Johnnie sprawled on the floor, covered in brown gunk, and we laughed. Then even Sadie started laughing and Myrt was barking, and we just couldn't stop. And we didn't want to stop because sometimes in life you have to ignore everything, ignore the killer drones and the deadly aliens and the exploding sewage. And just have a laugh.

And then we saw something walking towards us – and the laughing stopped.

It was small, no bigger than a three-year-old, and it walked on two legs. A spacesuit covered it from head to toe, and as it came closer we could see our faces reflected in the visor.

I'd stopped breathing – we all had – and then the alien pressed a button on the side of its helmet and the visor lifted up.

What I saw turned everything I thought I knew about aliens on its head. Because there's no better way of describing it than this: the alien . . . was the cutest little monkey you've ever seen.

'We need to kill it quick,' Sadie said, trying to push me out of the way.

'Why do you always wanna kill things?' I said, exasperated.

'It's got a banana,' said Johnnie.

'So what?' said Sadie.

I looked at the space monkey – it seemed to be offering us a banana, or maybe threatening us. It was hard to tell.

HOW TO FIGHT SOMEONE WITH A BANANA

The argument went no further than that, because suddenly the space monkey didn't need a weapon. In the blink of an eye we were surrounded by a dozen drones. And they had something infinitely more dangerous than a banana.

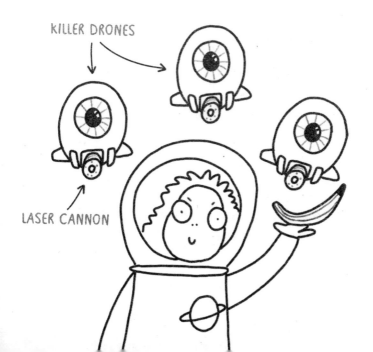

KILLER DRONES

LASER CANNON

The monkey waved its banana – as if to say 'follow me' – and then it frowned and poked the banana at us, as if to say, 'Or we'll shoot you.' At least I think it was saying that[21] – frankly, the laser cannons told us everything we needed to know.

Myrt started growling and Sadie looked ready to fight, but suddenly there were even more drones – behind us, above us, everywhere. Pincer claws reached towards me and it was all I could do to stop myself crying out in pain as a claw gripped tightly on to my left ear.

There are times to fight and times to give up, and this was definitely a time to give up. One false move and we'd have had our ears pierced:

---

21 There's a chapter in *The Book of Secrets* – **Secret 14: How to Have a Conversation with a Monkey or Baby** – but I've never read it. I never thought there'd be any point.

HOW NOT TO GET YOUR EARS PIERCED

We walked mile after mile in that inescapable ear grip. At one point I thought my ear was going to come off, but with those laser cannons pointed at us we didn't dare say anything, let alone ask questions. Then finally we turned a corner and immediately knew we'd reached our destination.

The room was enormous, and it was filled with screens and busy with activity. There were monkeys everywhere, dozens of them – and apes too – all shapes and sizes and species – some you'd recognize, some like you've never seen. But they all just ignored us. It was like we weren't even there.

'We're in the control room,' whispered Johnnie breathlessly.

The cute little monkey gave him a fierce look. But he was right: we were in the control room at the heart of the alien spaceship. And it was truly awe-inspiring:

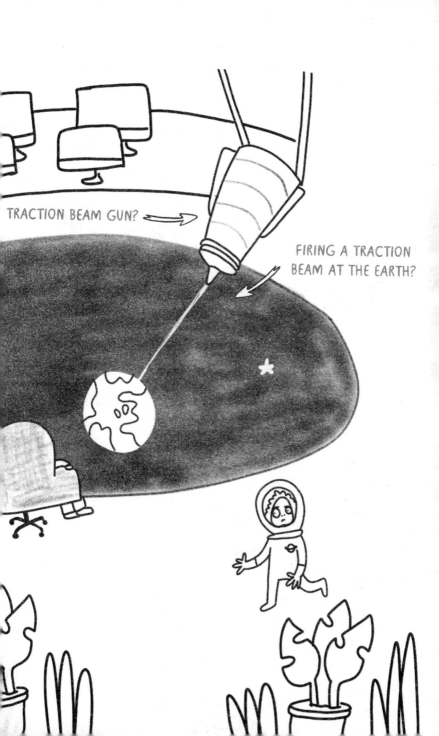

'Wow.'

That was Johnnie, but we were all thinking it. Well, maybe not Myrt, and probably not Sadie, but I was definitely thinking it.

In comparison the Earth looked small – a pale blue dot in the black of space. But I couldn't take my eyes off that big gun and the beam of red light shooting out of it. A 'traction beam', Karlos had called it. A beam to destroy every organism on the planet. I actually felt my heart sink then, actually physically, sink. It seemed to drop down into my stomach. This . . . was just too big. Nothing could stop this, and especially not me, a ten-year-old kid.

The space monkeys, or space apes, or whatever they were, looked busy – swiping left and right, and up and down on flashing screens. And they looked terrifyingly efficient.

I thought about what Mum would say if she

could see all this.

'Let me help.' That's what she'd say. It's what she always said – her gentle way of reminding me how useless I am. And she'd be right. This problem, it was just too big. We needed to forget it and concentrate on rescuing Mum and Dad.

I turned to Johnnie – he was jigging about from one foot to another. He only does that when he has a brilliant idea or needs the loo.

'Johnnie? D'you need to go?'

'A little bit.'

'Why didn't you go in the septic tank? We were right there. It's gonna be impossible to find something now.'

But if Johnnie did need to go he was obviously able to hold it for once. 'Look,' he whispered loudly, nodding towards the traction gun, 'it's a graviton gun!'

Now three of those four words I understood. But graviton?

I've learned from painful experience not to ask Johnnie questions, because one question leads to three more. And then nine. And eventually ends up with Johnnie lending you some of his books.

'What's a graviton gun?' asked Sadie. She had a lot to learn.

'It's a gun that fires gravitons . . .'

Sadie looked at me.

I just shrugged.

'What's a graviton?' she couldn't help asking.

'Gravitons are the bits inside atoms that make gravity work.'

I looked at Sadie with a face that said 'I knew this would happen', but she just wouldn't stop with the questions.

'So why are they shooting gravitons?'

Johnnie never got to answer. A voice from behind a giant gaming chair answered for him. It spoke perfect American.

'Just think of it like a big stick – a big stick made out of gravity – that's poking the Earth and stopping it from spinning.'

And then the chair belonging to the voice turned, and we saw who'd spoken . . . Not a monkey, not an ape, but a boy. A boy of about fifteen. And I must have let out a gasp or something because the boy was laughing at me. And he must have a laughed for a while because before he'd finished, I knew exactly who he was.

It wasn't just his big eye; it was everything – the smile, the glasses, the dodgy trainers, everything.

The voice and the laugh and the big eye all belonged to my deadly nemesis.

HOW TO CONFRONT
AN OLD ENEMY

'Noah?'

It was Noah, no doubt about it.

Except it wasn't.

It wasn't the middle-aged billionaire who I'd accidentally blown up in space in 2053.[22] And it wasn't the ten-year-old I'd accidentally blown out of an artificial volcano in 5000 BCE.[23] This Noah was a teenager, a proper teenager, with spots and an interesting hairstyle and everything. This Noah was all glowed up – he even looked cool. What is it about teenagers? They can't stop playing with their hair and grunting, but they do look cool.

---

22 See *How to Survive Without Grown-Ups*.
23 See *How to Survive Time Travel*.

Now, if you're like me, when you meet someone
you've accidentally blown up twice, the first bit of
conversation can feel a bit awkward.

'Hi,' was all I managed alongside a little wave.

'Hello, Eliza Lemon. We meet at last.'

Now that threw me. I looked at Johnnie and then back at Noah.

'You're another copy, aren't you? A clone,' said Johnnie.

Teenage Noah just smiled.

In case you haven't read my second journal,[24] this will take some explaining, so let me have a go. Here's a bit of background on Noah and his clones:

---

24 See *How to Survive Time Travel* (it comes with a free tip on how to have two summer holidays in a row).

A BIT OF BACKGROUND ON NOAH AND HIS CLONES

With Normal Time Travel

(if you can call it that): you obliterate yourself and then just send the recipe for making you down a wormhole back to whatever time or place you choose. (Think of it as a cut-and-paste job) . . .

But When Noah Does It:

he doesn't obliterate himself. (Think of it as copy and paste) And he's been doing it since he was a kid, so the upshot is there's loads of different Noahs around of all ages, shapes and sizes . . .

The Bad News Is:

there still seem to be quite of lot of Noahs out there trying to destroy humankind because Noah thinks Planet Earth is doomed to some horrendous doomy doom if he doesn't wipe out humans first.

The Good News Is:

this has really helped me get over the fact that I've blown up two of them. Morally it's like stepping on an ant vs stepping on a hamster.

'So you're still trying to wipe out the human race?' I heard myself saying.

Noah shook his head but didn't say a word. He just looked at me with his big eye (and his little eye, but it's the big eye that's weirdly charismatic).

'You're such a loser.'

This was from Sadie. She'd somehow managed to get her ear free from the killer drone's inescapable ear grip, but the drone now had the other ear in the same inescapable grip.

'Why can't you just leave humans alone?' Johnnie called out unexpectedly.

Noah finally answered. 'D'ya remember what I told you, Eliza?' Teenage Noah's voice seemed flat, almost lifeless. Like someone had got him out of bed way too early. 'Do you remember that I've seen the future? I've seen what happens to Planet Earth. To every single one of the million billion creatures.

Well, this is that future.' He paused, staring at the little blue planet. 'This is what I've been trying to avoid all these years.'[25]

'What happens to them?' asked Johnnie. He was starting to cry.

'They freeze and they burn,' said Noah without emotion. 'The Earth stops spinning and the pale blue dot turns half white with snow, and half beige with desert.'

Now this didn't make sense. If stopping the planet from spinning was so bad, then why was he doing it?

'Come see,' he said simply, and the drones dragged us forward – with that killer ear grip we

---

25 In case you're wondering how *this* Noah could know what a *different copy* of Noah told me thousands of years ago – so was I. How could the different copies of Noah know what each other had said and done? Well, Johnnie cleared it up later – Noah had obviously read my journals when they were turned into a super-successful series of books.

had no choice. They dragged us across the control room, right to the edge – where the beam fired into space.

'Careful,' said Noah. 'No health and safety here – one step and you're falling into empty space. But just look at the view.'

We looked through the red light at Planet Earth. It should have looked purple through the red, but it didn't. It looked black, like a planet of death. I thought of Karlos and all those people in their little cubes playing video games. And I thought of all the creatures busying about, going about their normal lives, totally unprepared for what was about to happen.

'Why do this?' I said and the drone gripping my ear squeezed tighter. I let out a howl of pain. 'Just tell me!' I shouted. 'Why are you doing this??'

Then I noticed something. Something I should

have noticed before. Noah turned up his hand and waved it at me. A funny, pathetic little wave because round his wrist was a metal band. And round his legs was the same metal.

'I'm not doing anything,' said Noah. 'I'm a prisoner – just like you.'

And for some reason my tummy twitched with fear. A great big spasm of fear.

HOW TO FACE FEAR

There's all sorts of advice: deep belly breaths . . .
holding your earlobes so your heart rate goes
down . . . eating sweets is supposed to help. Some
people say that eating a sherbet lemon is the best
thing of all. But we were all out of sherbet lemons.
Besides, Noah just wouldn't stop talking. And he
was getting properly worked up.

'Do you understand now? I've been trying to
stop this all my life!' He looked at the great gun
above us. 'This is what I've been trying all my life
to avoid. But nothing works – believe me, I've tried
everything. But something –' he looked me right in
the eyes – 'or *someone* always gets in the way.'

'You mean me?' I said. My voice had gone quiet.

'Yes, you, Eliza Lemon. You thought you were saving humans – when, in fact, you were saving them up . . . for a fate worse than death.'

I didn't know what to say to that. Everything I thought I knew was turned on its head. Noah had always said he was trying to save Earth by getting rid of humans. What if he'd been right? What if that was the only way to save the planet?

'So if you're the good guy,' asked Sadie, 'who's actually doing all this?'

Before Noah could answer the doors opened – the great double doors we'd come through minutes before. The drones fell back, and in ran row after row of heavily armoured apes. Their helmets glistened violet in the bright light, covering their faces. But we didn't need to see their faces to know we were in big trouble.

Finally, once the soldiers had blocked off the doorway, there entered the most terrifying thing that either you, I or anyone in the history of the galaxy has ever seen. He literally floated into the control room on a giant sofa – one of those fancy sofas that only has one arm.

'Eliza Lemon,' said Noah. 'Meet **THANIT**.'

HOW TO MEET THANIT

Back then I didn't know that the name '**THANIT**' would come to be known across the planet – across history. That it would be used by parents to scare their children: 'Get to bed . . . or **THANIT** will come for you!' or 'Eat your greens . . . or **THANIT** will get you.' I had no idea that children would lie awake at night, fearful of slipping into a dream in which **THANIT** *did* come for them.

To cut this short, even on a casual glance it was pretty clear to everyone, even Sadie, that **THANIT** was the bogeyman's bogeyman. If the bogeyman had kids – and for some reason those bogeykids were refusing to go bed – then the bogeyman would say, 'Get to bed . . . or **THANIT** will come.'

I didn't know any of that then. But I just had to look into his yellow bloodshot eyes, sunk deep into a head so fat that it looked like he'd been stuffed by a trainee taxidermist to know that we were all in the biggest trouble of our lives.

Still don't believe me? Then look at this:

Myrt growled next to my leg but quietly – I could feel it more than hear it. Sadie flexed her hands silently.

'Do monkeys normally have eyebrows?' she whispered.

'It's not a monkey,' said Johnnie. 'It's some kind of ape – but not like any ape on Earth. And, yes, monkeys do have eyebrows. They just don't call them eyebrows.'

'What do they call them?'

'They don't call them anything – they're monkeys.'

The ape raised his eyebrows and everything went quiet.

'**KNEEL!**' he roared, and the drones dragged us down by our earlobes until we were kneeling.

Then he smiled and raised a giant hairy eyebrow and the drones finally let go, flying two steps backwards,[26] leaving us kneeling and not knowing quite where to look. Only Sadie was left in an ear grip, like they somehow knew the rest of us were totally useless.

I, for one, was totally distracted by those eyebrows.

---

26 Johnnie, in case you read this, I know that doesn't make sense. But you get the picture.

HOW NOT TO GET DISTRACTED BY EYEBROWS

When you're trying to make peace with a superior alien civilization that has the ability to destroy all life on your planet, it pays not to be rude. Which is why Myrt's first response to this monster was particularly disappointing.

THANIT lowered his thick monobrow and his sofa drifted towards us.

'SO YOU ARE THE GUARDIAN.' He looked down at me. There was nowhere to hide and nothing to say, so I just nodded and tried to kneel a bit taller.

'Why are you doing this?' said Johnnie. He was looking upset.

'BECAUSE WE ARE DANSA – AND WE COME FROM PLANET DANSA TO CORRECT OUR MISTAKE.' The big ape's voice rumbled out of him like rocks tumbling under ocean surf.

'Dansa?' said Sadie. 'Where's that?'

THANIT lifted his head, scratched under his chins and then pointed upwards with his strangely mobile eyebrow. **'THE PLANET OF THE THREE SUNS. YOU KNOW IT AS PROXIMA B.'**

Johnnie nodded and Myrt started growling. I gave her a nudge with my knee.

'What have humans ever done to you?' I heard myself asking. But even as I said it I thought it sounded desperate.

THANIT'S eyes widened. **'BUT ARE YOU HUMAN? OR ARE YOU DANSA?'**

'What?'

He laughed at that – a great bellowing belly laugh that made his floating throne wobble in the air.

'HUMANS ARE A MISTAKE, AND I AM HERE TO CORRECT THAT MISTAKE.' THANIT looked at Noah sitting quietly now, still cuffed to his chair. **'TELL THEM,'** he said.

Noah nodded, clearly nervous. 'We're not humans. We are . . . *were* Dansa. Earth was never meant to be a home for apes. We don't belong here.'

'That just doesn't sense,' said Sadie. 'Humans evolved here on Earth, everyone knows that – from monkeys and stuff.'

Noah shook his head and looked out at the blue planet. 'Humans didn't evolve here. We were sent here.'

'But why?' My voice sounded quiet, even to me.

'BECAUSE WE SHOWED MERCY,' said **THANIT**. **'BECAUSE WE WERE FOOLS. AND MANY THOUSANDS OF YEARS AGO . . . WE GAVE YOU A SECOND CHANCE.'**

Noah looked at me. 'This is what I've been trying to tell you. Humans on Earth are a huge mistake. Back on Dansa we caused nothing but trouble, so they gave us one last chance – our own planet . . . Planet Earth to look after.'

And suddenly I understood.

Plant Earth wasn't really ours – this was just a test to see if we could look after it and stay out of trouble.

'But why come now? Earth looks perfect in 2525.'

I thought of all the cherry blossom and the happy people playing video games. 'Humans are doing better than ever before.'

Noah answered that too. 'In a few months humans will send out their first interstellar spaceship. In time humans will try to take over the entire galaxy. If the Dansa don't destroy Earth now, everything will just get worse. They think humans will put the whole galaxy in danger.'

'THIS STUPID EXPERIMENT,' said **THANIT**, his voice cracking like thunder, **'IT ENDS NOW!'**

'But, but . . . humans are civilized now! We're good and kind.'

I thought of Karlos and the people in their cubes. I thought of them sending Johnnie and Sadie – two children – up here to their deaths, just to save their own lives. Hmmm, maybe humans weren't any kinder or more civilized in the year 2525, after all.

'No, Eliza, we'll never be that,' said Noah – and he looked genuinely sad. 'It has to end now. If it doesn't, then things just get worse.'

'Worse?' My voice was deeper and louder. 'Worse than destroying all life on Earth?? What can be worse than that?'

But teenage Noah was shaking his head. 'I've seen even further into the future, a hundred years from now.' His eyes looked hollow and haunted. 'I've been there – if **THANIT** doesn't do this now, then the entire galaxy will be destroyed.'

'BUT I WILL DO THIS NOW,' said the gigantic ape, as if it needed pointing out, **'I AM THANIT, SAVIOUR OF THE GALAXY.'**

There was silence then. I looked at Johnnie and Myrt and Sadie, and they looked at me. But there was nothing any of us could think to say.

'SHOW ME THE TIME MACHINE.' The rumble

of **THANIT'S** voice broke the silence, and two monkeys pushed our sofa through the huge doors and into the room. There was silence until it came to a stop next to Noah.

I held my breath and calculated the distance between us and the sofa – it was our only chance of getting out of here alive. **THANIT** looked at the brown sofa too. He licked his lips like he wanted to eat it.

And that's when I realized something important. Whoever these Dansa were, they weren't quite as technologically advanced as I assumed. I looked back at Johnnie meaningfully.

They haven't mastered time travel. Surely that gives us an edge? Now is the time for you to apply that Big Brain, buddy boy. You think while I buy us some time.

But he just looked back like this:

WHA?

That's another thing about Johnnie – it's like he can't read expressions. He always thinks I'm annoyed when I'm not – and he always thinks I'm not annoyed when I am annoyed. It's so annoying.

'TELL ME,' THANIT said, deliberately looking at me. **'TELL ME HOW IT WORKS.'**

'Well,' I said with confidence I didn't feel, 'first, you need the remote and it's small and black and so well hidden you won't find it in a million years. A billion years. You'll need to look under every rock, in every stream and river. You'll have to take Planet Earth apart stone by stone if you want to find that remote.'

'Don't be dumb, 'Liza. It's the big rainbowy one now, remember?' Johnnie said as he pulled out the big rainbow remote from his trouser pocket.

'Johnnie! You're such an idiot.'

But I didn't need to say it. **THANIT** was laughing, a great rumbling roar of vibrating belly fat. Then he suddenly stopped, as if it wasn't funny at all.

'THE ONLY TIME MACHINE IN THE ENTIRE GALAXY.' he said simply, **'AND YOU'VE BROUGHT IT RIGHT TO ME.'**

One of the drones hovered towards Johnnie and he backed away, finally afraid, clutching the remote to his chest. But there was nowhere for him to go. Another step back and he'd be tumbling through the traction beam and into empty space.

'Just give it to them, Johnnie. Don't be a hero.'

He looked at me and then at Sadie, all the time shaking his head.

'But, Eliza, we *are* the heroes.'

'SEIZE THE REMOTE.' said **THANIT** almost

187

casually, and the drones started forward. But Johnnie was quick. He held up the remote and shouted to make sure he was heard.

'Stop!' His voice sounded desperate and I could see he was terrified. 'Or I'll chuck it.'

He looked back into the traction beam. Up close it was nothing like jam, more like a giant red river of light flooding out of the spaceship and crashing down to Earth. And then I saw something change in Johnnie's scared little face. A flicker of hope creeping at the edges of his mouth. A hint of a smile so small that no one but his sister would ever notice it.

But I did notice it and I knew immediately that Johnnie was about to do something. Something possibly very, very brilliant, but probably very, very dumb.

He took another step back – a step closer to the traction beam. The drones inched closer.

'Johnnie *don't!*' I screamed, not even knowing what he was going to do. But he just took another step backwards.

The red light behind him flickered and sparkled. Suddenly I could see on his face that he was going to jump.

'No, Johnnie! You *can't.*'

But a smile spread across his face, like it does when he's just solved a Rubik's Cube in his head. 'Eliza, it's OK. I was wrong; it's not a graviton gun. It's not firing anything,' he said, and he looked right at me. 'It's on *suck.*'

Then he fell.

He just fell backwards with his eyes shut.

And then he was gone.

THANIT bellowed a great ape roar and the drones went fizzing out into the void to give chase, but soon they were back – unable to follow Johnnie as he plummeted to Earth.

I was still on my knees – my brain splattered with thoughts of Johnnie – suffocating or freezing as he fell from space. If Sadie hadn't got her other ear free at that precise moment, who knows what would have happened.

But Sadie is a trained fighter – give her an inch and she'll take a mile, and then she'll rip your arm off. At least that's what she did to the drone.

The drone hit **THANIT** like a bowling ball. It bounced off his belly, but not before knocking his floating sofa backwards.

That all gave me the half-second I needed. In that half-second I made a decision: I had to save Johnnie. And if jumping out of a spaceship was good enough for him, then it was good enough for me.

I ran at the sofa and gave it a shove. Then I did something I've been doing all my life: I jumped on the sofa. Myrt was right behind me and then Sadie was pushing and only Noah, sitting there cuffed to his chair, stood between us and the abyss.

He tipped over his chair, trying to block us, but the sofa just slammed into him and it didn't slow a jot. Suddenly, with **THANIT'S** roar behind us, we began to tip and then fall. Myrt, Sadie, Noah in his big chair, the sofa, the lot.

I shouted as we fell, screaming into the void.

HOW TO SCREAM IN SPACE

They always say, *'In space, no one can hear you scream.'*

But what do *they* know?

I know, *for a fact*, that a scream in space is every bit as loud as a scream anywhere else. Sadie punched me on the arm until I stopped.

But as we continued to fall something didn't feel right. It just didn't feel as scary, *or as fast*, as it should have done. It was more like going down a slide covered in honey.

I held on to Myrt, and Johnnie's words came back to me. 'It's on suck,' he'd said. In the jumble of my mind I began to understand. Because what my annoying-but-sometimes-quite-useful genius brother Johnnie had worked out – and which would have taken me a year to figure out for myself – is that the traction beam wasn't shooting out of the doughnut at all.

The doughnut was sucking the beam in.

The traction beam was going **UP**.[27]

That, it turns out, is a really good thing if you

27 If you want to know how a traction beam can stop the world spinning and kill a billion billion creatures, you're probably a bit dangerous and you probably shouldn't be given this sort of information. But Johnnie insists it's really interesting, so, against my better judgement, here goes:

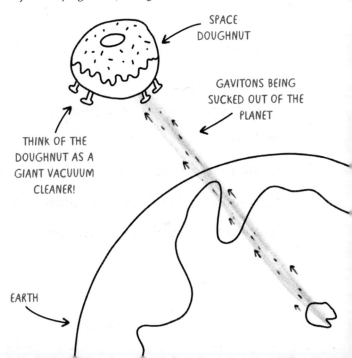

SPACE
DOUGHNUT

GAVITONS BEING
SUCKED OUT OF THE
PLANET

THINK OF THE
DOUGHNUT AS A
GIANT VACUUUM
CLEANER!

EARTH

want to skydive from space.

Because despite gravity's best efforts to smash us down to Earth, the traction beam was sucking gravitons upwards. And the net result, as we tipped over into the abyss, was something like this:

You think you know what falling feels like, but

you don't. You only know what *the first bit* feels like – the rushing sensation you get when you jump off a bed or a diving board. That rushing feeling is because you're getting faster and faster. But when you skydive, it's not like that at all. After that first bit, *you stop getting faster* – and then, well, it's the most peaceful, wonderful thing you'll ever do. It's like you're not moving at all – just floating.

Now that sounds great (and it was!), but all the time I was worried about Johnnie. He'd only jumped a few moments before we had, but in that time he'd travelled miles. I could see him right below us – just a little dot. Between us and him was Noah – still sat in his chair, eyes shut tight, like he was meditating

'Terminal' velocity is the fastest speed you can go because air resistance matches the force of gravity when you get to a certain speed.
J xx

It's also terminal because it kills you. That's the bit people need to know, Johnnie.

P.S. Stop writing in my journal. Next time I catch you even reading my journal, I swear I will wedgie you to death!

or something.[28]

After a few moments I started feeling travel sick, and then Myrt started playing up so I let go of her and just had to hope she wouldn't do anything stupid.

Finally Sadie spoke. She'd been looking obsessively back up at the space doughnut. 'Why aren't they coming after us?' she asked, and I immediately felt stupid for not thinking of that.

'Maybe they don't want to die?' I offered hesitantly.

'That's my other question,' said Sadie. 'Why aren't we dead?'

I obviously looked confused because she repeated the question.

'I mean, why aren't we dead from jumping from space without a parachute?'

Which happened to be quite a good question.

---

28 Which was weird. *What's he thinking?* I remember thinking.

HOW TO JUMP FROM SPACE WITHOUT A PARACHUTE

There's an Austrian guy, Felix somebody, who famously parachuted to Earth from space years and years ago in 2012. He had a **fire-proof spacesuit** so he didn't get burned to a crisp, and he had an **air-proof spacesuit** so he didn't die from lack of oxygen. And, most importantly of all for any parachutist, he had a **parachute**.

We had none of those things, and despite feeling a little bit queasy (which could easily be explained by my irregular mealtimes that day) and a little bit light-headed (too many lentils?) I basically felt very not dead.

'Maybe it's something to do with the traction beam?' I offered without much conviction. 'Johnnie would know – he'll have it all worked out by now.'

I looked down at the Johnnie dot below us. It was getting bigger. He'd spread himself out to slow his fall, helping us catch up.

'So you mean you jumped from the edge of space without knowing we'd be OK?' Sadie looked properly angry. 'You two are just total idiots! You could have killed me.'

Now I don't normally stand up to Sadie – you wouldn't either: she once wedgied a teacher for talking back at her – but for some reason, maybe lack of oxygen to the brain, I argued for once.

'Well, we didn't exactly have much choice, did we?' I argued.

'You can always fight, idiot.'

'Then why didn't you?? Why didn't you fight off

a million monkeys and killer drones and whatever that **THANIT** thing was?!'

Myrt growled, but Sadie ignored her.

'Because I'm not the hero, Eliza Lemon. I'm not the chosen one with the big statue that can be seen from space.'

'Why are you even here, Sadie?' I locked my eyes on to hers and refused to look away. She stared right back at me. I thought we'd be stuck like that, in a never-ending-blink-off, but then, maybe for the first time in her short, angry life – she looked away.

I couldn't believe it. I'd won a stare-off with Sadie Snickpick.

'I don't know,' she said angrily. 'Johnnie asked me. I thought it might be fun.' She was looking down at Johnnie far below us, and the Earth beyond. 'Besides, it was a right pain looking after him at school – he's totally clueless. He thinks he's there to teach the teachers. Mrs Crosse was going to lock him the basement and chuck away the key.'

I couldn't think of what to say to that.

Maybe Sadie had a heart after all, I remember thinking. It was like she'd adopted Johnnie as a little pet animal, but it all just seemed so unlikely.

I was getting a headache thinking about it, so I turned my back to her. Myrt wriggled round on to my lap and for the next little while I just sat there, looking down at Johnnie as he slowly got bigger and closer.

It was beautiful up there on the edge of space. And the smells . . . Imagine being in a swimming pool in the woods after a thunderstorm – well, it smells exactly like that. Don't ask me why, though Johnnie would know. And you can see for ever – the

It's the ozone – it's what you smell before a storm and it can sometimes be a bit chlorine-y, like a swimming pool.

J x x

moon is enormous for one thing, and the Earth? It really is like a giant blue beach ball – you just want to kick it, or punch it and watch it go boing.

But the blue beach ball was getting closer. And something my dad once told me popped into my head. I was only young but I'd tried to climb a tree at our local park. The one and only time I've ever tried to climb a tree.

'It's not the fall that kills you,' he'd explained. 'It's the bit at the end where you're hit in the face with a rock the size of a planet.'

HOW TO SURVIVE BEING HIT IN THE FACE WITH A ROCK THE SIZE OF A PLANET

All in all we fell for another hour.[29] By then several things had become clear. Some were kind of good, some kind of bad.

SOME GOOD THINGS	SOME BAD THINGS
Johnnie seemed happy.	Noah seemed even happier (what's he planning??)
Johnnie was close.	Noah was closer!
We weren't dead.	we might be soon!!
	ARE WE HEADING STRAIGHT FOR NOAH'S ISLAND???

---

29 Yes, an hour! No one ever believes me when I tell them that.

I still had Johnnie's telescope in my rucksack and, with my heart hammering, I pulled it out. Sure enough, we were headed straight for Noah's island. Of all the places on Planet Earth, what were the chances of landing there??

I have nightmares about that island – most weeks. The deadly animals, the creepy brain-burrowing robots, the booby traps, pitfalls and poison. The

It was actually more like fifty-five minutes. J x

whole island was a giant web of death – and we were the flies heading inescapably towards it.[30]

I shivered even though it wasn't cold. The island would be older now – much older, but from a distance it was just as I'd remembered it.

The pyramid-spaceship was obviously gone, but the giant lobster-claw bay with its delicious beach was still there. So was the endless rainforest with the mansion at the heart of the island. I thought of the

---

30   It's all in my first journal if you want to read about it. Yes, you know it already – the laugh-till-you-vomit *How to Survive Without Grown-Ups*.

giraffes saddled up and ready to ride and wondered what had happened to them . . . and the biobot millepedes ready to burrow into your brain while you slept, and the rows of robot bonobos endlessly tapping away at their computers. As we fell closer, I saw something else – our final destination – the source of the traction beam.

I squinted through the telescope, because at the back of the mansion was something I'd never seen before: a giant conservatory. It was like something from Kew Gardens but bigger. Like the world's biggest birdcage.

The blood-red traction beam was surging out of a round skylight in its roof. A hole maybe too small for our sofa to fit through, I remember thinking. But suddenly Johnnie was flying into view. He was trying to get my attention.

I had no clue what he was saying, but the next moment he had his school jumper off and was pointing at it meaningfully. Then, without more warning, he turned it into the world's worst parachute, and I immediately understood.

It was time to slow down.

HOW TO SLOW DOWN

The thing about a rubbish parachute – and Johnnie's parachute was probably the rubbishest parachute since Mary Poppins used her totally unrealistic umbrella – is that it still does *something*. And when you're both falling down a traction beam it didn't need to do much for us to catch up with Johnnie.

He went shooting past teenage Noah (still meditating in his chair[31]) and he would have gone flying past us too – except Sadie has the reactions of a mongoose. She reached out and dragged him on to the sofa and suddenly he was jabbering away and Myrt was licking him and I just smiled into his chubby little face.

---

31 Seriously, what was Noah thinking about all this time??? He was definitely planning something, BUT WHAT????

'Johnst, we need to use the time machine now – before we crash,' I said quickly, holding his arm to make sure he didn't fly away.

Johnnie shook his head. 'Don't be silly. We can't use the time machine while we're falling.'

'Why not?' asked Sadie, grabbing the rainbow remote control off him. I was glad I wasn't the only one who didn't understand all this time-travel stuff.

'Yeah, why not?' I repeated.

'Two reasons,' said Johnnie. 'Reason one: the calculations will be all wrong – we'd risk sending back just our feet. Or just our heads.'

Now that seemed like a good enough reason all on its own. But Sadie clearly wanted to hear Reason 2.

'What's the other reason?'

'The other reason is this.' He waved at the ground, clearly expecting us to understand, but we didn't.

'This what?' said Sadie.

'This. Earth. We can't just leave it. We have to save it.' He looked me in the eye. '*You* have to save it.'

That was the cue for another argument right there. It was like he'd forgotten that our number-one priority was getting back so we could save Mum and Dad. But we never got the chance to argue, because just then a giant gaming chair came smashing into my back and I went tumbling into empty air.

We'd made a fatal mistake. We'd forgotten that Noah – even a teenage Noah – was a total evil genius.

HOW TO FIGHT OFF A TOTAL EVIL GENIUS

Even though I was tumbling around, I could see that Noah had Sadie by the arm and was trying to get the rainbow remote off her.

Johnnie and Myrt, just like me, had been knocked for six. They were clinging on to each other – but spinning about, totally out of control as they were flung through the traction beam and into the empty sky beyond. They immediately plummeted to the Earth at a shocking speed. And I knew my only job was to save them.

If you've ever been skydiving, you'll know how easy it is – right up until the point when it becomes impossible and you lose total control and spin about and lose all sense of up and down. When that happens your only hope is that you don't vom until after you've died from smashing into the ground.

I narrowed my shoulders and, tipping my head, shot after them.

The sudden acceleration as I left the traction beam was terrifying. The wind made my eyes stream and I struggled to see. I couldn't help but notice the island beneath us. Suddenly it was growing at a horrifying rate. With every blink it doubled in size.

And then, with Myrt and Johnnie almost close enough to grab, I saw our chance. If we could just land in the sea – feet first – there was just a chance we might survive. Wasn't there?

HOW TO LAND
ON YOUR FEET

I made a grab for Myrt's tail, then Johnnie's foot came right up in my face and I held on to it with my other hand, pulling him towards me and pushing down his little legs.

'We need to land feet first,' I shouted, but there was no way he could hear above the noise of the wind and the sound of his own screaming. So I just pulled him close, hugging him tight, with Myrt tucked between us.

We hit the water seconds later – and it felt like concrete. I was sure I'd broken my ankles, and then I was sure I'd drown because we were just going down and down and down. I opened my eyes in panic, but what I saw made me shut them again.

And then, after what felt like an age, we finally stopped – *deep* underwater.

And then, after a terrible pause, we were shooting upwards – faster and faster until the sea popped us out like little human corks. As we went flying up, Sadie came crashing down right on top of us. And then we were together, holding each other in a circle, with Myrt doggy-paddling between us. Everyone was grinning – even me.

The shore was close, and I soon had a faceful of sand (if you've ever jumped out of a spaceship without a parachute you'll know the first thing you want to do when you reach it is kiss the ground).

It was warm on the little beach and almost exactly as I remembered it. The water lapped gently across the sand and the coconut palms gave plenty of shade. Rock pools invited you to sit and watch as tiny fish played in the shallows. The ice-cream kiosk had disappeared; a faded plastic sign was the only clue it had ever existed. A thick hedge with purple flowers formed a boundary against the jungly interior, and, all put together, the beach felt like the safest, cosiest place you could ever be. The sun was halfway to the horizon[32] but the sand still held the heat of the day. No one spoke for many minutes and I just sat there pushing my fingers through hot sand, watching Myrt as she danced about in the surf.

I sat there wishing we could hide here for ever. That all this mess would just disappear: the space doughnut, the alien apes, the traction beam, the statue, everything. Some days I want to be a dog, allowed to snooze all day in my basket. And sitting on that beach, in the warm sand, I felt like that times a million.

Johnnie was busy with his telescope, but

---

32 Johnnie explained it to me later – we'd obviously travelled west, so the sunset hadn't happened there yet. Or east. Or something. I can't really remember.

West! J xx

eventually Sadie broke the silence.

'Noah got the sofa,' she said simply. 'But he didn't get the remote.'

She held up the rainbow remote control for our time-machine sofa and nodded to herself in satisfaction. 'He's also got a black eye,' she finished.

I wondered which one, the big eye or the small, but then decided it didn't matter.

'Where did he land?' asked Johnnie. 'Did he stay inside the traction beam?'

Sadie nodded. She was smacking a coconut against a rock and it split after two hits.

'Then he'll have landed right on top of the mansion,' I said, my throat tightening at the thought of going back to that terrible place.

'We head for the mansion, then,' Sadie said, swallowing coconut water. 'Ready?'

I wasn't ready – I never would be ready. Not to

go back there. But as I looked at Johnnie, I knew we had no choice. If we wanted to get the sofa, and get back to save Mum and Dad, then we had no choice.

And then, at a shout from Johnnie, I realized something else. He was staring into the sky through his telescope and I snatched it away. The space doughnut was spilling little multicoloured dots. In my imagination they were like hundreds and thousands, but through the eye of the telescope it was immediately clear – the dots were

monkey-shaped.

'Space monkeys!' said Johnnie.

And I knew he was right.

'OK, people,' said Sadie, 'let's get a wriggle on.'

HOW TO GET A
WRIGGLE ON

Johnnie, being the genius sort of five-year-old he is, had timed our fall from the space doughnut, 'Out of scientific interest.' By Johnnie's calculations we had exactly fifty-five minutes and thirty-eight seconds before the space monkeys smashed into the conservatory at the back of the mansion.

'Fifty-five minutes and a handful of seconds to save the world,' he said.

'Fifty-five minutes to save our skins,' corrected Sadie.

I couldn't help but think of Mum and Dad again – Dad literally frozen, and Mum stuck in the year 5000 BCE. If we could just get to the sofa we still had a chance to save them.

Fifty-five minutes to save Mum and Dad, I thought, but didn't say out loud.

Sadie was immediately all action and, using her boot, made a hole in the hedge. She entered the rainforest without a backwards look. Johnnie followed and then Myrt. Knowing there was nothing else for it, I too entered the jungly interior of Noah's island.

We headed straight north and made quick progress. Sadie was at the front, ripping a path using her arms and legs, and we covered ground quickly. She was like a machine. With his weak left leg Johnnie could barely keep up – even though Sadie was the one doing all the work.

The jungle seemed noisier than I remembered. A troop of howler monkeys were arguing somewhere far away – and a non-stop hum of insects filled the air. We must have covered a mile in that first sprint through the forest. We would have kept going – Sadie would have just kept going for ever, I think – if she hadn't spotted the pawprint.

'Pfssst,' she hissed, holding up an arm to signal a halt. Then she crouched and we could see what had made her stop: a giant pawprint five times the size of Myrt's and freshly made in the damp mud.

'Just look at that,' she said, pulling a single black hair from within the pawprint. 'Isn't that just the biggest jungle cat you ever did see?'

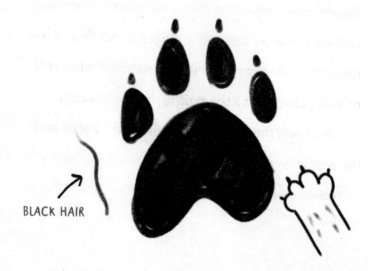

BLACK HAIR

HOW TO TRACK A JUNGLE CAT

The Book of Secrets has a chapter on this, but I've never read it. It's one of those secrets that you assume you'll never need. Like, How to Ride a Tiger Shark and How to Stop Eating Chocolate.

But Sadie clearly *had* read it.

'Black panther,' she said quietly, 'but bigger. Bigger than anything I've ever seen.' Then she cocked her head and put a finger to her lips. The message was clear, and we listened for almost a minute. Listened to the pulsing hum of insects.

And then the pulsing hum just died away and the jungle went suddenly silent.

Not just *quiet* but silent.

Utterly silent.

And that can only mean one thing.

TOP 5 CREEPIEST THINGS

#5 Silent jungle.

#4 Old people who take their teet out and pretend they want to kiss you.

#3 People who can turn their eyelids inside out.

#2 Finding a toenail in your yoghurt.

#1 Babies who can speak.

WHAT TO DO WHEN A JUNGLE GOES UTTERLY SILENT

There's only one reason why a jungle goes utterly silent. And it's not a good one.

In every jungle there's one animal, one *predator*, that's deadlier than all the rest. One predator that *everything* is scared of.

And when *everything* is afraid, *everything* goes quiet.

Once you know why a jungle suddenly goes silent, a silent jungle is the creepiest thing there is.[33]

---

33 Except maybe babies who can speak. Actually, now I think of it, a silent jungle only just scrapes into the top five. But you get the point. It was creepy in a scary way.

Whatever they were all afraid of, we knew it was close when even the butterflies stopped flapping. They literally crashed to the ground – because that was better than being eaten.

I looked at Johnnie, and his face said it all.

I turned to Sadie; her hands were curled like claws. If this was a giant black panther, she was ready to fight.

When you're in a life-and-death situation like that, you start hearing things – things that sound like a giant black panther creeping about. At first

you're not sure. Then you look at Sadie and she has
a face like this:

And then you look at Johnnie and he has a face
like this:

JOHNNIE'S
WIBBLY FACE

And then you hear another noise that **just has to be a giant black panther**.

And you have half a second to think, *Maybe* the next noise I hear will be the sound of my skull being crunched in a panther's jaws? And then someone screams: 'RUN!' and then you realize it's *you* screaming.

AND THEN YOU RUN.

Dolphins run as fast as a horse? Don't think so.

Johnnie x

HOW TO OUTRUN A GIANT BLACK PANTHER

If you look them up in a book, most animals run about as fast as a horse. Don't ask me why, it's just what books always say. Hippos, giraffes, tigers, kangaroos, camels, pet rabbits, zebras, even dolphins. They all go about as fast as a horse. Probably giant panthers do too. The only animal that doesn't?

Humans. They run about *half* as fast as a horse.

And the only animal slower than a human?

Johnnie.

Sadie was off and gone in a heartbeat. But Johnnie? There was no way he was going to outrun this thing. I turned to him, and it looked like he'd had the exact same thought.

'Johnst,' I whispered loudly, 'we have to fight.' I picked up the nearest thing I could find – a rock the size of a pebble. It wouldn't hurt a butterfly.

I imagined hitting the panther right in the eyeball. But even in my imagination the panther's eyelashes just batted it away.

'Johnnie, have you got anything we can fight with?'

Johnnie had his backpack off, rootling around as if we were settling down for picnic.

But it was all too late.

First came a **crack**. The unmistakable crack of a stick being trodden on only metres away – just the other side of thick undergrowth.

I didn't know where to look. Would it leap high in the air and come crashing down on us? Claws

A rock the size of a pebble is a pebble.

Johnnie XX

out, scraping our guts out with a single swipe of its paws? Or would it come stalking along like a pet cat after a ball of wool?

Then came a **thud**.

'Did you hear that?'

Johnnie nodded. 'It sounded like . . .'

But he didn't need to finish. It was obvious what the thud sounded like.

It sounded like a dead giant black panther thudding to the ground.

And without stopping to think *What could kill a giant black panther?* we went to have a look.

HOW TO SURVIVE SOMETHING THAT CAN KILL A GIANT BLACK PANTHER

I'm not really sure what I was expecting to find.

The giant panther just lay there, slumped on the forest floor like it had been hit by a stun grenade.

'Do you think it was hit on the head by a coconut?' said Johnnie. He was right behind me, stuck like glue.

'Don't be stupid. What are the odds of that?' Sadie was back, right behind Johnnie.

How does she move so fast? I remember thinking.

But only for second, because then they started arguing.

'It's not stupid.' Johnnie looked annoyed now. 'coconuts kill more people than any other fruit.'

'Now that is triple-decker stupid. Stupid One: coconuts kill dumb humans, not highly evolved apex predators with nine lives and the reflexes of a jungle cat. Stupid Two: no coconuts.'

She pointed upwards and, sure enough, no coconuts.

'And Stupid Three: it's a coco*nut* not a coco*fruit*. The clue's in the name.'

I could see Johnnie's mouth opening, but before he could say, 'That's the funny thing, a coconut is, in actual fact, a single-seeded fruit,' his mouth snapped shut.

His eyes grew wide and I spun round to see what he'd seen.

And there it was.

Sitting on the panther's stunned head.

The cutest little creature you've ever seen.

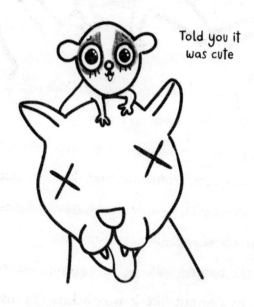

Told you it was cute

'What is it?' said Sadie. She was by my side now.

I couldn't answer. I couldn't do anything but look into those giant brown eyes. They just seemed to grow bigger and bigger the more I looked at them.

'It's soo cute,' someone said, but I'm not sure who. It could even have been me. All I could do was look into those enormous brown eyes.

Its little tongue was the only thing that moved; it went in and out like it was licking an invisible lollipop.

Without meaning to I took a step closer. And then another. Sadie was still next to me, reaching towards it, and I was suddenly terrified that it would run away before I got a chance to hold it. It was just sooo cute.

'Eliza, don't!'

Johnnie's voice made me jump and I turned, annoyed. 'What's your problem now?'

'I know how the panther died.' Johnnie looked properly frightened, but it just made us laugh.

'You think that little thing killed it?'

He nodded. 'It licked it to death.'

I turned back to look at the little animal. It was just sat there, its tongue moving slowly in and out.

'It's a slow loris,' said Johnnie. He said it like he was saying, 'It's a ninja zombie' or 'It's a karate vampire.'

Sadie snorted. 'I'm glad it's not a fast loris. You'd be filling your pants.'

But even as she said it, I couldn't help noticing that the loris was now sitting on her shoulder. I hadn't seen it move a centimetre, but it was now on her shoulder.

I was immediately jealous but Johnnie let out a gasp. 'Sadie, it's on your shoulder.'

Sadie looked surprised, and then cross-eyed as she twisted her neck.

And that's when I noticed a second slow loris looking out from a tree, and then another and another. Loads of them . . . all staring with their giant brown eyes. All licking invisible lollipops.

All unbelievably, unbearably cute.

'Sadie!' Johnnie's voice was shaking. 'Don't let it lick you.'

'Lick me?? Why would it wanna lick me?'

'Its saliva's venomous. It's the deadliest spit in nature. And I think these have evolved into predators. One lick and you're dead.'

I could suddenly feel my heart jumbling around in my chest.

'Sadie,' I said, trying to sound calm, 'Johnnie doesn't get this stuff wrong.'

The grin fell off Sadie's face. 'So what do I do?'

'Just don't get licked,' said Johnnie.

HOW NOT TO GET LICKED

Have you ever played Weeping Angels?

Basically, some people are the angels and they can't move when you're looking at them. But look away, or even blink, and they can **get** you. And if they get you, you're dead and become one of them. And you keep playing until **everyone's dead**.

Well, slow lorises, it turns out, are a lot like that.

'Just keep looking at it. As long as you're looking at it, you're safe,' said Johnnie.

Sadie's neck was twisted at an impossible angle as she locked eyes with the loris.

It sat there looking right back, licking the air in front of her.

Sadie stared at the loris and the loris stared back.

Time seemed to stand still.

It was a blink-off . . . **to the death**.

HOW TO WIN A BLINK-OFF
(TO THE DEATH)

'Don't worry, Sades,' Johnnie said, reaching into the side pocket of my rucksack, *The Book of Secrets* has a chapter on this one.'

He pulled out *The Book of Secrets* and flicked through the pages at speed. Then he read:

'**Secret 191: How to Win a Blink-off** . . . Blah blah blah. This is it, Step 1 . . . Close your eyes for a minute before you begin.'

'Johnnie, get to the good bit . . .' shouted Sadie.

'Um . . . um . . .' Johnnie's lips moved as he speed-read. 'Yep, yep, this is it. Think of something really sad – the tears will moisten your eyes and—'

'Like what?'

'Anything – anything sad.'

I immediately thought of Mum the last time I'd seen her in 5000 BCE – all alone and ancient and with no one to smile with or talk to. No one to cuddle when she felt sad or afraid. I'd never thought of it before, but even grown-ups feel sad and afraid sometimes. I felt tears prick my eyes and I gritted my teeth, determined to banish them. But it was already too late. Because while Johnnie had been fumbling around with *The Book of Secrets*, and while Sadie and I had been staring at the loris, our little bit of jungle had gone from this one moment:

Wide-eyed for the blink-off

Wide-eyed in panic

THE BOOK OF SECRETS

To this the next:

There were slow lorises everywhere. There was even one on my hand. It was pricking my skin with its little claws. And suddenly it wasn't cute. It was creepy

'I think I know how to win a blink-off,' said Sadie.

'How?' I said, my hand beginning to shake.

And then she punched the slow loris. Right in the face.

'Run!' she bellowed.

And we ran.

HOW TO OUTRUN A SLOW LORIS

Even Johnnie managed it.

I thought they'd chase after us, especially after what Sadie had just done, but they didn't even move.

We ran through the jungle not caring where we were heading. Just anywhere to get away from those creepy little tongues. We kept going until Johnnie couldn't go any more.

'Slow down!' he shouted.

He was angry. He always is when he can't keep up. Sometimes I just ignore him, but this time I didn't.

'You're going the wrong way,' he said, staggering along like a marathon runner in the desert. 'The mansion's that way, I think.'

'You think?' Sadie said, unimpressed.

'Wait, let me check something,' said Johnnie.

A moment later he had his little mini-compass out and, head down, started walking sideways into the undergrowth.

'Don't go far,' I called out, but he seemed not to hear. Myrt followed and I was soon left alone with Sadie. She had a boot off and was picking something out from between her toes.

'I hate leeches,' she said, squeezing one between her fingers. There was another on her ankle and she flicked it off. I yelped when it landed on my trousers. Sadie looked up in disgust.

'You're such a wimp.' She spat the words at me. 'Why don't you just give up now and save us all a lot of time?'

I thought it was just an insult, but she kept staring at me.

'I mean it,' she said. 'Why don't you ever give up?'

'What do you mean?' I asked nervously, wondering where this was going.

'At school, when I twist your arm or push you over, your face looks like you wanna kill me. But you never fight back. Why?'

'I dunno, maybe I know when I'm beaten,' I said with a deliberately stupid smile.

'No, you don't. You never look beaten.' Sadie picked off another leech from the back of her leg.

I wondered what she meant by that. But I kept my mouth shut and eventually she spoke again.

'The other kids, sooner or later, they all know. When they're beaten, I mean. You can see it. Their eyes. They stop looking me in the face. They laugh before I've even finished telling a joke. But not you.'

I didn't laugh. And suddenly I realized I was looking at her face. I wanted to stop, but for some reason I couldn't.

'You just look at me as though . . .' She trailed off, but not for long. 'No matter what I do to you, you always look at me like you've won. Because you'll never give up.' She shook her head then and watched me warily. 'You're such a loser, Eliza. But you're the **Loser Who Never Gives Up**.'

I tried to give a little modest smile.

'You know Johnnie thinks you're going to save everybody? For some reason he thinks you're a hero. But you're not – you're just a loser. And as soon as we find that sofa I'm getting out of here.' She held up the rainbow remote control to make her point. 'With or without you. You understand?'

Johnnie came back then, looking more lost than ever.

'Oh,' he said, 'I thought you were over there.'

Sadie took one look at his compass and rolled

her eyes. The little arrow was wagging about like a dog's tail.

'For heaven's sake, do I have to do everything?' she said, and started climbing one of the trees. She climbed it as fast as I climb stairs and soon disappeared among the branches. Moments later a loud whoop told us she'd reached the top.

'We're close!' she said. 'I was right – it's this way. Come on.'

And then, I kid you not, she literally jumped – using the leaves and branches to slow herself just enough to avoid breaking anything. She landed like a superhero. And in that moment I was more certain than I'd ever been before . . .

Sadie was not a normal human being

SADIE SNICKPICK *VS* **NORMAL HUMAN BEING**

SUPERHERO
LANDING POSE

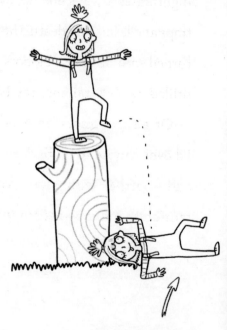

2 BROKEN ANKLES
+
BROKEN EVERYTHING
ELSE

We followed her quietly after that, and she led the way to the mansion.

And even though we walked my heart started to quicken. Because the mansion is the place my nightmares always end up, even now. It's a place of traps and lasers and death, the place my parents were turned into brainless biobots and a robot millipede drilled its scaly tail into my baby brother's head.

Of all the places on Mother Earth it's the last I'd ever choose to go back to. I held Johnnie's hand and, together with Myrt, we walked through the rainforest and towards our worst nightmare.

HOW TO FACE YOUR WORST NIGHTMARE

Sadie had raced on, but we soon caught up with her, standing on the edge of an immaculate lawn. The mansion was straight ahead of us and she looked at it as if she was mesmerized.

I remembered seeing it for the first time myself: an oasis of mown grass and clipped hedges surrounding the grand timber-frame house. All surrounded by jungle, all hidden by the jungle.

The pets were all gone – the giraffes, the zebras and the giant turtles swimming round the little moat. But unbelievably there was still a lawnmower working with a monkey driving it carefully up and down to create perfect stripes of lawn.

The house had seen better days – it was now half covered in an avalanche of trumpet vines, but it was unmistakably the place of my nightmares.

But Sadie wasn't interested in any of that.

'Look,' she whispered, pointing to the conservatory at the back of the house. And immediately I saw it – the time machine, our sofa – our only way out of this hideous, inescapable mess.

It had smashed into the roof of the giant conservatory, almost blocking the traction beam coming out of the skylight in the conservatory roof.

'It's just sitting there,' said Sadie with a smile, 'waiting for us.'

But first we had to get to it – and that meant going back into the mansion. Just the thought of that made my stomach squirm.

I smiled at Johnnie and he smiled back at me, but inside I was screaming at the idea of going back inside.

'What's the plan?' said Johnnie, but he wasn't asking me.

'We climb that tree,' said Sadie. 'Get on the sofa and get out of here.'

'But it's a monkey puzzle tree?'

'So?'

It was my turn to speak. 'So it's a called a monkey puzzle tree because even a monkey can't climb it.'

'So?' said Sadie.

'So . . . Johnnie's got a weak leg – he couldn't even climb into a bunk bed.'

HOW TO CLIMB A MONKEY PUZZLE TREE

The Chilean evergreen tree *Araucaria araucana*[34] is even harder to climb than it is to pronounce. Its triangular leaves are so thick and so sharp that even goats won't eat them. And they lose their branches as they grow – leaving a slender branchless trunk at the base.

Sir William Molesworth was the first person to bring the tree to Britain, in about 1850, and he famously won a bet with the local zoo – challenging them to find a monkey who could climb the tree and eat the banana he'd placed at the top. Upwards

---

34 You say it *Aroo-care-ee-a aroo-carn-ee-a*. Or you can just say 'monkey puzzle tree' like everyone else.

of thirty monkeys tried and failed to climb the tree – and so it became known as the monkey puzzler, and eventually, the monkey puzzle tree.

I looked at the tree – and doubted that even Sadie could climb it, let alone me and Johnnie.

'OK, losers, you waste time going through the house, I'm taking Route A.'

She looked into the sky and we did the same. The parachuting monkeys were still in perfect formation and they were close now – I could see them clearly even without Johnnie's telescope. My heart fluttered at the thought of them arriving before we reached the sofa.

'But, Sadie, you have to come with us,' said Johnnie. 'We need you to destroy the traction beam.'

Sadie put a hand on Johnnie's shoulder. 'Johnsty, give it up. It's too dangerous. There's an army of space monkeys coming for us. We've got ten minutes if we're lucky.'

For once Sadie and I agreed.

'Come on, Johnst,' I said. 'This isn't our fight. We get to the sofa and we get away whilst we still can. We have to go back and save Mum and Dad – they're more important. We have to go home.'

But Johnnie's eyes were filling with tears and I knew this was going be more difficult than I thought. 'No, Eliza – we can't just let the planet die. Think of all the animals.'

As if to prove a point, a little baby bird landed on the lawn near us.

We both watched Myrt growl

at it, but the little bird just kept pecking the lawn, unafraid. And then Johnnie looked back at me.

'We just have to destroy the traction beam. You've got the pineapples, remember? And the sunflower seeds and the skipping rope. **The computer** said we just have to use them.'

I thought about the pineapples in my rucksack, with the sunflower seeds and the skipping rope – and immediately felt uncomfortable.

'Johnnie, listen to yourself, what are we going to do? Make a fruit salad and some bird food?'

'Maybe,' said Johnnie. 'I don't know yet, but we have to believe in ourselves.' He nodded towards the baby bird on the lawn and said, 'Finches love sunflower seeds more than anything. Maybe if we feed them they'll help us?'

But it didn't take a zoologist to know what a stupid idea that was.

'Johnnie, look at it – it's smaller than mouse. It must weigh less than **THANIT'S** eyebrows. Just believe me, there's nothing we can do – it's too late.'

I looked at the sun hovering low in the sky in a perpetual sunset. It hadn't moved since we'd arrived on the island. 'The planet's already stopped turning.'

'But I've worked it all out!' Johnnie gave me a hopeful little smile. 'If we can just use the mini-black hole to suck down the gravitons in the traction beam—'

'They'll just send down another one.'

Johnnie's face brightened. 'No, that's the brilliant thing.' He started fumbling in his pocket and pulled out a scrap of paper. 'The mini-black hole also sucks down the space doughnut and swallows it up and the sudden jolt gets the planet moving again – gets it spinning again.'

I must have looked blank because Johnnie pushed

the paper in my face. Even Sadie took a look – and there, all sketched out with Johnnie maths, was a plan to save the Earth.

How to Save the Planet

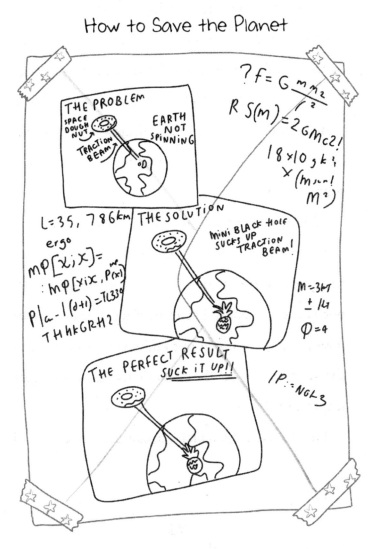

'Did you work all this out when we were falling from space?' I asked, but the shaky handwriting told me the answer.

Johnnie smiled proudly.

'And then what?' Sadie interrupted.

'Well, once we've saved the planet, we get on the sofa and go home and rescue Mum and Dad.'

'Johnnie,' I said, 'just listen to yourself – you're talking about saving the planet with a black hole. It doesn't work like that.'

'It will work,' he said desperately, stabbing his finger at the maths on his little bit of paper.

Sadie grabbed it off him, screwed it into a ball and tossed it over her shoulder. She looked proper angry. 'I only agreed to come here because I thought it would be a laugh, but from the first millisecond people have been doing everything they can to smash us, laser us and lick us to death. I've had enough. I'm done here. Do you hear me?!'

'Please . . . we have to try,' Johnnie said, looking from Sadie to me and then back again.

'You do that, little man,' snorted Sadie, 'but if you're not on the sofa by the time those monkeys arrive, then I'm outta here.'

We looked up again at the falling monkeys, but this time something was different. I lifted the telescope for a better look and what I saw took my breath away. I only had a second before Sadie snatched the telescope from me, but the image is still in my brain whenever I shut my eyes and try to sleep. Because it wasn't just monkeys falling to Earth.

THANIT was coming too.

Sadie took one look through the telescope and then dropped it on the lawn. I saw fear on her face.

'I don't want to leave you behind,' she said, holding Johnnie by his shoulders, 'but I will if I have to. If you're not on the sofa by the time that thing lands, then I'm gone. D'you understand?'

And then, without another word, she was off – running like a sprinter towards the monkey puzzle tree at the back of the house.

I looked at Johnnie. His eyelashes were wet with tears and I knew I had to say something. 'All right, we can try. OK?'

Johnnie forced a smile.

'Just one try – that's all. We have to get on that sofa, because we're the only chance Mum and Dad have got.'

Johnnie didn't say anything, but he nodded.

'OK, you heard her,' I said. '*Go-go-go-go-go!*'

We ran across the lawn in silence, Johnnie struggling to keep up. Myrt led the way up wooden steps to a large shaded veranda, and then in through the front door. The place where my nightmares always seem to start.

HOW TO GET OVER
A NIGHTMARE

Nightmares are funny things.

For all the sights and sounds and sheer blind panic, there's one thing you never have in a nightmare: **smells**.

No one ever smells anything in a nightmare.

Scientific fact.

And so when we stepped inside the mansion and smelled the musty damp air of the hallway inside – I knew immediately that this was real.

When we'd been here before the room had been filled with robot bonobos –

bonobobots,

Noah had called them. They sat in row after row, tapping away at keyboards. We never did find out what they were typing.

The noise of those clicking keys echoed in my ears as we stepped inside the gloomy hall.

'They're still here,' whispered Johnnie.

The bonobobots are always in my dreams – though in my nightmares they stop typing and they all look up at me and then, well . . . that's usually when I wake up – screaming. But here now, they just kept tapping away – as if we weren't even there.

I patted Johnnie on the shoulder and then pointed to the back of the hall – between the two sides of the double staircase was a door; it was green.

'That green door – it must lead to the conservatory.' I nodded to make sure he'd understood.

But before we could take another step the oddest thing happened. The bonobobots, who'd been typing away for nearly five hundred years, suddenly stopped. As if we'd triggered something just by stepping into the room. And then one by one they slumped forward on to their keyboards, as if desperate for a well-earned break.

All except one. The chimp nearest us. He looked right at me, but it was like he was trying to look *through* me, and then with one hand he pressed two keys on his keyboard.

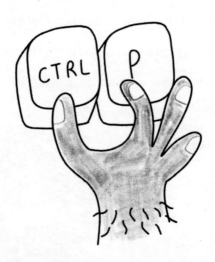

The familiar clatter and clunk of a printer clicked into life. It sat all alone on a table at the side of the room. We saw the paper judder, first in, and then out. But only halfway out, because at that moment it jammed to a halt.

HOW TO FIX A PAPER JAM

Only old people print stuff off. I've never understood it. It's like trying to use a horse to pull your car. And they spend most of the time swearing at the printer. You've probably seen them, cursing under their breath and yanking out ripped pieces of A4. Well, I have no idea how to fix a printer because I'm not old. And neither does Johnnie. But we ran over to it anyway.

Johnnie tore out the paper and studied it carefully. Finally he handed it to me with a shaking hand. 'You wrote this,' he said with an even shakier voice. 'You really need to read it.'

And I immediately knew that my life would never be the same again.

I should never have gone through the green door. I know that now. As soon as I stepped through that door, Johnnie was doomed. I'll never see him again, and that thought is the first one I have when I wake, and the last one I have as I cry myself to sleep.

My heart started racing even before I understood what I was reading.

'Is this what I think it is?' I read it a second time and then turned to Johnnie. He looked like he wanted to cry. 'Is this really *my* journal?' I thought of the notebook in my rucksack – I'd barely started writing it. 'One I haven't written yet?'

Johnnie nodded, tears spilling over his cheeks.

'But I don't understand . . . How can it be? If I haven't even written it yet? How . . .'

I trailed off. It didn't need Johnnie to explain it. We were in the far future – the year 2525 – so everything I'd ever written had already been written.

'I think the bonobobots are trying to warn us,' said Johnnie, and suddenly my brain was spinning as I tried to work out what this all meant. If I had written in my journal in the future, then it meant I had survived. It meant **I was destined to survive**.

But it also meant that **Johnnie**, by the sounds of it, **wasn't**.

And that meant we had to do something that Johnnie says is almost impossible: *we had to change our destiny.*

HOW TO CHANGE
YOUR DESTINY

The ancient Greeks believed in the Fates, three weaving goddesses who took a strand of thread for every human and wove it into the great tapestry of life. On the day each child is born, their destiny has already been decided. Nothing we do or choose will make a difference – it's all already decided.

That's what the ancient Greeks thought. But they also thought that you could cure toothache with a boiled earthworm,[35] so they weren't the brightest if we're honest.

According to Johnnie, though, when it comes to fate and destiny they were *mainly* right.

---

35 It's true – they put the boiled earthworm in your ear. They also thought the desert was full of giant gold-digging ants. Bit stupid, those ancient Greeks.

'Your life is a river,' he'd explained once, 'that is heading to the sea.' And while its course may not be fixed – it takes a lot to shift its path. A few tons of metaphorical gunpowder, in fact.

I looked at his quivering chin and tried to remind him of what he'd once told me. 'We can change this,' I said.

But Johnnie was shaking his head. 'How? It's already written.'

I scrunched up the paper and threw it, missing the bin. 'Nothing is written, Johnst; we just have to change your destiny.'

He was properly crying now and I hugged him, and Myrt jumped up and tried to bite us, as if we were somehow leaving her out.

Johnnie always seems tiny when he's crying. I used to be annoyed when he cried – Mum and Dad would go rushing over to make a huge, big fuss. But not any more, not since . . . not since they weren't around to make any kind of a fuss.

'Johnnie, it's easy,' I whispered into the top of his head. 'We just don't go through the green door – if I don't go through the green door, then I can't write that in my journal. That's what the bonobobots are trying to tell us: don't go through the green door.'

But he was pushing me away. 'You're right, 'Liza, you can't.' He stiffened his little body, trying to look brave. 'But I have to. I have to do this. If I don't go through that door, then no one will save the planet.'

I wanted to scream at him and struggled to keep my voice calm. 'Johnnie, you can't do this alone – it's too dangerous.'

He knew I was right, but he argued anyway. 'It'll be fine. Sadie's in there – well, on the roof – we'll do it together. And then we'll come back on the time machine and get you.'

I shook my head. 'This isn't a computer game; you don't just lose a life. You lose them all – for ever.'

I think he could tell this was an argument he'd never win because then he nodded sadly. 'I have to try, Eliza. Whatever happens, I have to try.'

He reached out for the rucksack and I handed it to him. Then he reached in and pulled out the pineapple-shaped waste-disposal unit.

'It's hard to believe there's an actual black hole in there,' he said, shaking it.

I didn't know what to say, and he was already walking away, Myrt following at heel.

'I have to go,' he said. My big rucksack looked ridiculous on his little shoulders, but he sounded more grown-up than I've ever heard him. 'The monkeys will be landing any minute. You mustn't worry, Eliza – once I've done this, we'll come and get you . . . with the sofa.'

He reached the green door and turned the handle, pulling the door towards him so I couldn't see anything but a red glow across his face. And then he turned to me for the last time.

'Sorry, Eliza, but I have to try.'

I wanted to scream *'No!'* and I wanted to say, 'There has to be a better plan than this,' but before I could say anything, they'd gone, closing the door behind them.

I collapsed to the floor; every ounce of energy leaked out of me. I was alone, sitting on a mouldy carpet with my head echoing empty thoughts.

I breathed a deep belly breath and tried to focus my brain. I had to stay focused, I told myself. I couldn't give up. *If I could just* **not** *go through the green door*, then maybe Johnnie's destiny would be changed. Maybe the river of Johnnie's life wouldn't have to end. There had to be another way into the conservatory. I just needed time to think.

But right at that moment I heard a scream – Johnnie's scream. The scream he uses when it's a matter of life and death. And mainly death.

Without another thought I was running – running to the green door.

Sometimes the Fates will get you whatever you do – the ancient Greeks believed that only the cleverest of the clever could ever outwit the Fates.

Which meant, as I ran towards that door, I had about two seconds to think of something really, really clever.

HOW TO THINK OF SOMETHING REALLY, REALLY CLEVER

I'm blessed with a brilliant imagination. I can literally see anything right before my eyes. I just have to think it and – *pop* – there it is. A pink hippo? No bother. Mrs Crosse crossed with a pink hippo?? Even easier.

It's also my curse. I can see how things will go wrong before they've even started going wrong. I live in the imagination of my future. Living through disasters time after time, all before they've ever even happened.

But every now and again, my imagination gives me the answer.

As I ran towards the green door, my imagination answered the call and suddenly **I knew a way.** A way to get through, without going *through*.

I didn't have to go through the door at all – I just had to crash through the wall. After almost 500 years of damp and mould, the plaster and the wooden timbers would be rotten and crumbling – and in my imagination it was all so easy:

Sadly my imagination is often totally wrong. And whoever built the house had taken the necessary steps for avoiding damp rot.

I bounced off the wall and landed with a bone-crunching smack. And then Johnnie was screaming again and Myrt was barking on the other side of the wall.

I scrambled to my feet and I had no choice. The Fates had decided our destiny, and there was nothing I could do.

Knowing that I would regret it for the rest of my life, I opened the green door and stepped through it. One way or another Johnnie was doomed – and there was nothing I could do to stop it.

All I could do was try.

HOW TO TRY

I stepped into the hot red light of the conservatory and for a moment I couldn't see. Johnnie was shouting and I blinked to focus. It was like I was inside a giant birdcage, birds everywhere and plants climbing up iron pillars. And there, right in the centre and looking like a giant pineapple, was the traction-beam machine – pumping gravitons (or whatever they were) into space. The red glow made brown shadows on the green tropical leaves.

Then I heard a laugh – the type of laugh only a teenager can laugh – deep and high and scratchy all at the same time. It was Noah – he was chucking birdseed at Johnnie and Myrt, and they were being attacked by tiny little birds.

It was immediately obvious they were losing.

I thrashed at the birds with both hands, but they were everywhere.

'Just give up, Eliza Lemon!' Noah's mocking shout made me look up. 'They're *vampire* finches. You can't win.'

'Why are you doing this?!' I wanted to scream, but I was too busy flapping at the swarming birds. They were on me now too – their claws biting into my skin.

And then Sadie shouted from the roof. I hadn't even noticed her. 'Get up here, you morons! They're *coming.*'

I looked to see Sadie perched on the sofa, which was still wedged into the conservatory roof. She was waving the sofa's remote control, and beyond her, now terrifyingly close, were the paratrooping space monkeys.

I didn't know it then, though I should have guessed, but vampire finches live on blood. They're the most vicious small bird in nature. And as they pecked at my hands and head and face, I sank to my knees, desperate to get away.

'Give up, Eliza Lemon!' said Noah, and I buried

my head in my hands and kneeled low to get away from the vicious little beaks and claws. 'This has to happen,' he shouted. 'If the Dansa don't do this now, then the whole galaxy is doomed. The more you try to save humanity, the worse it gets. Believe me. You've just got to GIVE UP!'

HOW NOT TO GIVE UP

You probably think I'm exaggerating, but I'd sooner face a giant black panther than those vampire finches. Once they taste blood it's like they go into a frenzy. A feeding frenzy – where you're the meal. Think of a bunch of five-year-olds at a birthday party – well, it was like that – and I was the cake.

And that would have been it – The End – I would have ended up as bird food. But just then – with a bird literally trying peck into my earhole – I remembered . . . *Finches love sunflower seeds more than anything.* That's what Johnnie had said.

'Johnnie, the birdseed . . . in the rucksack.'

I didn't see what happened next – I couldn't really even hear it. With my head down between my knees, birds swarming over the back of my head, I couldn't really hear anything – just my heart thumping.

But I could imagine. I could imagine Johnnie reaching into the rucksack for the pot of sunflower seeds that Karlos had given us. I could imagine him flinging them far and high.

And it must have happened like that, because suddenly the birds were gone – I looked up to see them swarming after sunflower seeds. Johnnie, bless him, had managed to fling them right in the face of teenage Noah.

And now it was Noah's turn to be cake.

'You remembered?' shouted Johnnie, and he was grinning and Myrt was barking.

'Remembered what?' I shouted back.

'About sunflower seeds – that they're a finch's favourite food?'

For a second I laughed. I laughed out of pure relief.

But only for a second. Because one more second later, Sadie started screaming. A big bellowing scream.

'SPACE MONKEYS INCOMING!'

'Johnnie,' I cried out, 'get that pineapple black hole into the traction machine.'

The first space monkey was already smashing through the conservatory roof. Then a second, then more. Glass shattered everywhere, hailing down on top of us. It was a rain of terror slicing through the air.

HOW TO SURVIVE A
RAIN OF TERROR

Waves of glass crashed on to us and it was a miracle we weren't sliced up. My head went down again and I hunched over Myrt as the glass thundered down to the tiled floor. But if shards hit me, they just bounced off. By some chance in a million they just... bounced... off.

As the last of the glass fell, I looked up carefully and immediately regretted it.

There were monkeys everywhere – and up close they were truly terrifying.

A monkey paw smacked Johnnie to the ground and he went skidding across the tiles, but he clung on to the pineapple like his life depended on it. I screamed at him to get up – and he half did – but another smaller monkey leapt on to his back, pinning him to his knees.

And then I saw the rainbow remote crash to the tiled floor. Sadie had dropped it. I watched it crack open – wires and batteries spilling out. Myrt dived after it, and for a second I thought she was going to bring it to me.

'*Myrt, go fetch!*' I cried, but it was hopeless – Myrt has never retrieved anything in her life. She just grabbed the remote in her mouth and began to chew. And as she bit through the wires and the circuits – all hope of escape evaporated.

We were doomed; we were stuck here in the future for ever.

But there wasn't even time to give up. Johnnie was in trouble. He held up the rucksack like a shield, but the space monkey swatted it away. And as the rucksack slid to a stop by my foot, I watched the space monkey grab Johnnie's throat – squeezing the air out of him.

Then I noticed the rucksack and the skipping rope spilling out of it. And I knew what I had to do.

HOW TO USE A SKIPPING ROPE AS A NUNCHUCK

In kung fu lessons they don't let you practise with nunchucks until you reach black belt.

There's a simple reason for that: most people, when they use nunchucks for the first time, hit themselves on the back of the head.

I knew all this – I'm not totally stupid – but the skipping-rope nunchuck was the only weapon I had, and I was the only chance Johnnie had. Besides, some inner Jedi voice spoke to me . . . it *told* me . . . to *use the skipping rope*.

So I did.

The wooden handle smacked me on the back of the head. A truly eye-watering bang to the brain. And the world around me began to blur.

A LONG TIME IN THE FUTURE

So here we are. It's a long time in the future, the year 2525 to be exact. And things are bad. Really bad.

Now you know why I'm in a giant birdcage fighting off space monkeys who are trying to wipe the entire human race off the face of the Earth. And you know why my baby brother, Johnnie, is trying to open up a pineapple – so he can save the planet with a mini-black hole.

And you also probably know that it's all utterly, utterly hopeless. With Myrt chewing on the remote there is no escape. The only thing that could save us from being eaten by vampire finches is being destroyed by space monkeys first. And the only thing that could stop the space monkeys is a mini-black hole. And Johnnie couldn't even open the pineapple-shaped waste-disposal unit, let alone toss it into the traction-beam machine. He's a terrible thrower.

I looked through the coils of skipping rope that had wrapped themselves round my head. I saw

Johnnie with the monkey on his back, struggling with the pineapple. I saw Myrt gnawing on the remote like it was a dog chew. I saw Sadie stuck on the roof, fighting two monkeys and trying to bite a third through its spacesuit.

'*Johnnie!* Just chuck it in the machine!'

But Johnnie was on his knees; he looked at me in despair.

'You know I can't throw that far,' he shouted. 'You're the hero, Eliza – do *something*!'

At that moment I'm sure you'll understand when I say that **I was absolutely convinced things couldn't get any worse**.

But then **THANIT** smashed into the roof of the conservatory. He smacked on to the sofa, the iron roof finally gave out, and everything came crashing down. Sofa, Sadie, **THANIT**, space monkeys, everything.

And there, amidst all the dust and chaos, I

started crying – properly crying. Tears flooded over my cheeks. It was at that point, I realized ,you can never really run out of tears, just like you can never really run out of love or hope or spit.[36] Tears are important. Tears tell us something; they tell us we're afraid, sad or angry. They tell us to risk everything or to hide or fight. Without tears we're just robots running on code. Tears make us human. And tears make us strong.

All the mayhem blurred away with those tears, and suddenly I felt some peace. For one brief moment it felt like I was just watching and all this hideous chaos was happening to somebody else.

And that precise thought was what gave me the idea.

Sometimes in life the difference between failure

---

36 I'm not sure why I wrote that, but it's true – if you try *not* making spit, you just make extra spit. Try it.

and success isn't being a superhero. It isn't about being somebody else – it *isn't* about being something you're not. **It's about being true to who you are**.

And that's when everything suddenly fell into place. I didn't need to be some superpowered superhero to save the planet.

I just needed to be myself.

HOW TO BE YOURSELF

A hero, even a superhero, isn't amazing at everything. Spider-Man can't fly, Wolverine is rubbish at giving head massages. Iron Man? Bet he can't even swim a width without going rusty. And that guy in *Guardians of the Galaxy*? Have you seen him dance??

They don't need to be brilliant at everything. They don't even need to be good at anything (look at Robin[37]). They really just need to be able to do one thing: to keep going, to **Not Give Up**.

Have you ever watched a superhero movie where the superhero gives up? No, neither have I. And you never will.

---

37 In case you've never seen a Batman movie – Robin is a total bullet magnet. He basically never does anything apart from get captured.

The thing is, not giving up is something anyone can do. It's something *everyone* can do.

And it's something I'd spent my whole life doing. Even Sadie knew it.

I'm the **Loser Who Never Gives Up**, remember?

Anyone *can* do it. But it's not easy. Not giving up can be pretty hard. You need a *lot* of practice, which is why you need to *fail* a lot.

I know this because I've spent my whole life failing. I've had more practice at failing than anyone in the known universe.

I've failed at just about everything.

All the time.

Every hour.

Every minute.

Fail, fail, fail.

Do you know how many times I've played netball in PE?

Neither do I, but it's been loads of times. And over the years I've only ever **lost**. I've not even come close to winning – not even fifty points close. I lose because no one ever picks me, so I have to play as a team of one. If you've ever tried to score from goal defence you'll know why that's never gonna work.

Except that in Year 5, I started practising long shots on goal, just to see if I could do it. And now I score at least once every match, sometimes twice. The last time we played, I only lost 54–2.

For some reason that popped into my head as I watched Johnnie collapse under the weight of the space monkey, as I watched Myrt chewing on the broken remote, and Sadie trying to bite **THANIT** though his spacesuit. It's an odd thing to think of at a time like that – netball, I mean – but then I'm convinced our brains always have a reason when they plop weird thoughts in our heads.

And suddenly, as I wiped away my tears, I knew what my brain was trying to tell me: **don't give up**. Eliza Lemon can score goals from goal defence. Not many ten-year-olds can do that. I should be the one trying to throw the pineapple into the traction machine, not Johnnie. Johnnie should be fixing the remote control, not Myrt. And she should be biting **THANIT**, not Sadie. And Sadie? Why was she fighting with her bare teeth when I had a perfectly good nunchuck wrapped round my head?

My brain pinged with the answer.

If the question was: **How do you save the planet from marauding space monkeys when all is definitely lost?**

Then there could only be **one answer:** SWAPSIES

Swap teeth

Swap nunchuck

Swap pineapple

Swap broken remote control

SWAPSIES

HOW TO SAVE THE PLANET FROM MARAUDING SPACE MONKEYS WHEN ALL IS DEFINITELY LOST

I unwound the skipping rope with increasing speed – if I could just get it to Sadie, anything was possible. Sadie Snickpick can stop a charging rhino with a Brussels sprout – imagine what she could do with a nunchuck?

Actually, don't imagine it. You don't need to – because I threw the skipping rope and she caught it just like that. Two seconds later, I got to see exactly what Sadie Snickpick can do with a nunchuck:

She whacked away space monkeys like they were helium balloons. The monkey on Johnnie's back flew so far, it landed next to Myrt. She dropped the remote and bit down hard.

I grabbed the pineapple off Johnnie and threw it at the machine – with two hands. The secret is to get loads of height and get lucky. But the more practice you get, the less luck you need, and after five years of playing on a team of just me – I didn't need much luck.

As soon as it left my hands, I knew it was going in. Netball's funny like that – you always know when a shot's going in.

I turned to Johnnie with a smile. He had the remote in his hand – somehow he'd managed to fix it in the time it took me to throw the pineapple.

'Get on the sofa, Johnst,' I said. Because suddenly I knew everything was going to be just fine.

Everything's Going to Be Just Fine

THANIT crashed backwards just as the pineapple flew into the traction-beam machine. Lights started flashing immediately. The machine wobbled, like it was trying to chew on a toffee, and then a great fountain of liquid came spurting out.

The liquid splattered on to my face, stinging my eyes when I shut them too late. My eyes burned and the smell of fruit told me why.

The liquid on my face smelled unmistakably pineapple-y.

'Johnnie, you idiot. You got the pineapples mixed up!'

HOW TO SORT OUT A
PINEAPPLE MIX-UP

'Where's the rucksack with the other pineapple?' I shouted at Johnnie. But it was long gone. Lost in the chaos.

'Get on the sofa, you two!' Sadie shouted from behind me and I backed towards her. **THANIT** was up on one knee shaking his head – he wouldn't stay down for long. The space monkeys were circling us, wary of Sadie's skipping rope.

And then I saw the rucksack. Noah had got hold of it somehow. He was hiding under a giant banana palm, the bag clutched to his chest, his big eye wide with fear. Sadie must have seen him too because her skipping rope came flicking out.

Noah screamed as the wooden handle cracked on to his knuckles and the rucksack fell from his grip. The pineapple bin came tumbling out and rolled across the tiled floor towards Johnnie.

'No, Johnnie, just get to the sofa!' I screamed, but it was no use. Johnnie fiddled with the remote control and then tossed it to me.

'You get on the sofa, Eliza,' he said simply. 'I've set the timer for ten seconds.'

I didn't know what he meant, but then a little computerized voice from inside the remote spoke, and I immediately understood.

'**Ten**,' said the voice.

'We can't just leave,' said Johnnie. 'We've got to destroy the space doughnut – it's the only way to keep Earth safe.'

'**Nine**,' said the voice. It sounded like a creepy, little, robot gremlin.

I would have grabbed Johnnie then. I would have

dragged him with me on to the sofa, dragged him to safety – but I couldn't. Because Noah slammed into me with his shoulder and all the wind came out of me as my head tipped back and we crashed on to the sofa.

'**Eight**,' said the remote.

I thought my head had come off. Noah had flattened me, and I struggled under his weight.

'**Seven**,' said the remote. Noah tried to rip it out of my hand, but I wouldn't let go. Sadie was shouting above us, there were monkeys everywhere, and I could see **THANIT** was about to charge. Like a massive, silverback gorilla he towered over everyone and everything.

'**Six**,' said the remote.

I elbowed Noah in the belly and he let go with a grunt. I slid off the sofa and got to my knees. Johnnie had the pineapple in his hands.

He twisted open the lid and I saw him throw it.

It bounced off the edge of the traction-beam machine. It bounced twice, right on the rim, and I got to see the black hole swirling about inside it. Then I saw the pineapple drop into the belly of the machine, just before Noah yanked me back by my shoulder.

'**Five**,' said the remote, and the familiar whir of the time-machine engine started up.

'Johnnie! Get to the sofa!' I screamed through the pain. And then **THANIT** was crashing down on top of us. Flattening everything.

'**Four**,' said the remote.

What happened next was indescribable – mainly because I was squashed beneath a scrum of fighting bodies. But I'll try.

The traction-beam machine started shuddering just like before. Except this time, with a thumping

BOOM, it collapsed in on itself. Until all that was left was the pineapple spinning on the floor, sucking on the red traction beam like a child sucking on jam.

And somewhere high up in space the doughnut spaceship was being dragged down with it. Just like Johnnie's maths had said it would.

'**Three**,' said the remote, now muffled under the press of bodies.

The traction beam was disappearing into the pineapple and the more it sucked, the stronger it became. Plants, pots, metal, glass, even monkeys were dragged towards it – like a tornado sucking everything into its path.

Johnnie smiled at me – just as the remote said, '**Two**.'

And finally he started to run.

But he was slow.

I saw him tugged backwards – as if by a giant

invisible hand. And then I felt the pull of the black hole. Time seemed to slow down. The massive **THANIT** was dragged across the floor like he weighed nothing. The sofa tipped and suddenly we were all sliding across the tiles – Myrt, Sadie, sofa, Noah, everything. The whole fabric of space and time seemed to stretch and bend as we slid towards the roiling black mass at the heart of the pineapple.

'*One,*' said the remote, as the space doughnut came smashing through the last remnants of the conservatory roof.

And then, impossibly, it disappeared into nothing. It was sucked into the pineapple black hole spinning on the floor.

I felt a jolt. As if the entire planet had been kicked into life.

I saw Johnnie smile. His plan had worked – the Earth was saved.

'We did it,' his smiling lips seemed to say. But I never heard the words. The whine of the time machine had become a squeal, and the world around us began to disappear. Like it was being rubbed out by a giant eraser.

And then everything went a sudden comforting black.

EDITOR'S NOTE

Eliza's third journal ends at this point. It arrived on my desk – out of the blue – at the end of last year. Also included in the package were some loose pages – pages that look like they've been ripped out of Eliza's fourth journal. Pages that suggest that there's almost certainly more to come in Eliza's story.

We debated whether to include the additional pages. We have ultimately decided to publish them, but with a **warning**: because what comes next may be worrying for more sensitive readers.

If you like happy endings, please stop reading now.

But if you want to know what happens next, and if you feel ready to read it, take a deep breath and prepare yourself. And, remember, no matter how worrying things get, there's always hope.

And one thing we know for absolute certain is that Eliza Lemon herself will never give up.

Sadie, Myrt and I got back yesterday at midnight 5th September 2053. Exactly the right time, but exactly the wrong place. We missed our garden by a few kilometres and landed right in the middle of the school — in the staffroom. There were space monkeys everywhere — at least five, and Sadie thinks six.

They ran, but who knows where. And who knows what they'll do next. Even just five space monkeys from a super-advanced future civilization can probably do quite a lot of damage. But I can't really make myself care about that. I can't really make myself care about anything. Because it only took me seconds to realize the most awful thing.

Johnnie hadn't made it back with us.

I should never have gone through the green door. I know that now. As soon I stepped through that door, Johnnie was doomed. I'll never see him again, and that thought is the first one I have when I wake, and the last one I have as I cry myself to sleep.

Sometimes I imagine what it's like to lose an arm or a leg – I imagine it aches where the empty space is. And that's how it feels to have lost my little brother. The whole world aches.

We're sure we saved the future – everything worked like Johnnie said it would. It's just Johnnie who wasn't saved.

There's surely no possible way he could have survived that black hole.

I couldn't sleep – so I stayed up all night and wrote my journal. And then the sun came up for my eleventh birthday, my worst birthday ever. No Johnnie, no Mum – she's still stuck in 5000 BCE. Dad seems Ok, but he's still in the freezer and it's really playing up. It makes noises like an angry chicken and I don't know what I'll do if it stops completely and he starts thawing out before I've got all the right medical stuff ready. But at least one parent's nearly back to being normal.

And it was **BACK TO SCHOOL** today, back to bullying teachers and double maths and PE. I had to go – because if I don't, then everyone will find out that I'm all alone. And then I'll be forced to live with Grandma and then there'll be no chance of unfreezing Dad and rescuing Mum. I just keep thinking that if anyone can rescue Johnnie from a black hole it's Mum and Dad. And so that's exactly what I'm going to do.

Mrs Crosse has signed me up for a new after-school club – Toilet-cleaning Club. I'm here now with all the other losers, all the kids whose parents will basically sign them up for any after-school club just as long as they get free childcare. I'm writing this in the boys' toilets – in

Cubicle 4 – pretending to unblock a really gross toilet.

But most of all I'm writing this because something incredi-weird happened today – and I'm not sure if I'm going mad – or if it means something really important.

To celebrate my birthday the school lunch menu was changed to 'Just Vegetables'. The school cook does it every year to make sure the whole school hates me, and – trust me – it works. You have to choose five vegetables from a list of six: cabbage, peas, sprouts, aubergine, extra cabbage and kale. Even I hate myself after eating that.

But that's not the point. The point is,

I chose peas as one of my vegetables. And even that's not the actual point. The actual point is that while I was sitting there chewing on my extra cabbage – the peas started moving. At first I thought my eyes were going funny. I'm pretty tired today. But then I was sure it wasn't just my eyes – because the peas were trying to tell me something.

I know, I'm going nuts, right?

And that's why I need to write this all down. To get my head together – to get my head round the whole pea thing. Because I need to draw the peas before I forget exactly what they looked like. Because if I'm right, if the peas really were talking to me, then there's only one person in the universe who could have sent me that message. And it means that Johnnie's not as gone as I thought he was.

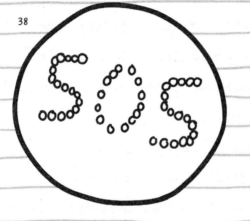

38

---

38 You might think it says 'So five', but trust me - it's 'SOS', as in 'Save our Souls'. It's exactly what Johnnie would write.

EDITOR'S NOTE

There was one more page. It arrived shortly after the first set of pages, and it was obviously written in haste later that evening. We're not completely sure what it means, but we've included it for completeness and because it offers, well, it seems to offer some hope.

ACKNOWLEDGEMENTS

The whole is greater than the parts and one of the delights of writing books is slotting into a team effort filled with professional brilliance. Katie Abey deserves to be made World President. And my editors deserve time off for good behaviour. Thank you Arub Ahmed, Lowri Ribbons and Ali Dougal. And huge thanks to my mind-bogglingly good: proofreader, Anna Bowles and copy-editor, Jennie Roman. The design team has transformed this into something wonderful. Thank you Jo Garden for your magic in creating the most gorgeous layouts and Sean Williams for another most excellent cover design. Thank you one, and thank you all.

LOOK OUT
FOR ELIZA AND
JOHNNIE'S FIRST
ADVENTURES

- AVAILABLE NOW!